UNDETECTED

TREASURE HUNTER SECURITY #8

ANNA HACKETT

Undetected

Published by Anna Hackett

Copyright 2018 by Anna Hackett

Cover by Melody Simmons of BookCoversCre8tive

Edits by Tanya Saari

ISBN (ebook): 978-1-925539-51-6

ISBN (paperback): 978-1-925539-52-3

Beneath a Trojan Moon – SFR Galaxy Award Winner and RWAus Ella Award Winner

Hell Squad – SFR Galaxy Award for best Post-Apocalypse for Readers who don't like Post-Apocalypse

The Anomaly Series – #1 Amazon Action Adventure Romance Bestseller

"Like Indiana Jones meets Star Wars. A treasure hunt with a steamy romance." – SFF Dragon, review of *Among Galactic Ruins*

"Strap in, enjoy the heat of romance and the daring of this group of space travellers!" – Di, Top 500 Amazon Reviewer, review of *At Star's End*

"Action, danger, aliens, romance – yup, it's another great book from Anna Hackett!" – Book Gannet Reviews, review of *Hell Squad: Marcus*

Sign up for my VIP mailing list and get your *free box set* containing three action-packed romances.

Visit here to get started:
www.annahackettbooks.com

CHAPTER ONE

D arcy Ward was having a really bad day.

As the plane she was on plummeted toward the ground, she wondered which god she'd angered. She gripped the armrests of her seat, her knuckles turning white. She should be gliding smoothly and happily back toward Washington, DC, but no, instead she was going to die a horrible, fiery death.

This was *not* how karma was supposed to work. She scrunched up her nose. Early this morning, she'd helped rescue her good friend, Sloan, and Sloan's new, hot-guy boyfriend from some very bad people. The plane bounced, knocking Darcy against the seat.

Fucking Silk Road. The black-market antiquities thieves who'd gone after Sloan—the same ones that Darcy was currently setting a trap for in DC—had clearly decided to retaliate.

She looked out the window. Smoke was streaming from one of the private jet's engines. The plane dipped again and her stomach ended up in her throat. She glanced toward the cockpit.

Special Agent Alastair Burke's broad back blocked the doorway as he leaned in, barking orders at the pilots.

Okay, well, if she was going to die, looking at Agent Arrogant and Annoying's mighty fine ass in his black suit trousers wasn't the worst way to go.

Another bump and she swallowed against the rock in her throat. She didn't want to die. She loved her parents, loved her brothers and her friends. She loved the business that they ran together—Treasure Hunter Security. Sure, her job consisted of mostly herding around former Navy SEALs-turned-security-badasses, but it was her life, and she loved it.

And she still had things she wanted to do. She wanted to fall in love, and be the center of some amazing man's universe. She wanted love like the love she saw every day between her parents.

Fucking Silk Road. The group had been the bane of her existence for a while now—well, the second bane of her existence behind a bossy, sometimes-ally-but-always-pain-in-her-ass FBI agent.

"Burke," she yelled. She wasn't going to sit here like a damsel in distress while they crashed into the ground.

"Quiet," he bit back.

He'd taken his jacket off, and was just in his crisp, white shirt and shoulder holster. Damn him for looking so hot while they were in danger of dying.

"Stabilize the plane," he growled at the pilot. "Now."

"The explosion knocked the system offline," one of

the pilots answered. "There's power, but it's not responding."

"Fuck," Burke muttered.

Screw this. Darcy's plans did not include being smushed into a million icky pieces. She unbuckled her seatbelt and grabbed her tablet.

She kicked off her heels and staggered down the aisle. The plane was tilted at a crazy angle. The aircraft bucked like a bronco and she lost her balance, careening into the cockpit.

Strong arms caught her and she looked up. Alastair Burke wasn't handsome, but there were a bunch of other words that she could use to describe him: hard, focused, rugged, intense.

Green eyes, that looked seriously pissed off, stared down at her, and her gaze fell to the stubble on his hard jaw. He had scruff even though it was the morning.

"I told you to stay strapped in."

God, the man was bossy. "And I didn't listen to you. Again. Surprise!" She looked at the console. Yikes, it looked like something you'd find on the space shuttle. "I thought I could help."

"You know how to fly a damaged plane?" Burke drawled.

"No." She held up her tablet. "But I am a genius with all things electronic, remember? I hacked your fancy, secure system, didn't I?"

He scowled. "I hacked you back."

She barely resisted the urge to poke out her tongue. She preferred *not* to remember that. She looked at the harried pilots. "What's going on?"

The head pilot glanced at Burke before looking back at her. "There's power to the console, but the controls aren't responding."

"Reboot it," Burke said.

The copilot shook his head. "It'll take too long. We'll have crashed by the time it comes back up."

Darcy dropped to her knees between the pilots' seats. "Let me see what I can do."

She plugged in her tablet and tuned out the pilots' frantic talk with a control tower somewhere. She also blocked out the whine of the engines, the jerking of the plane, and Burke's annoying, yet delicious cologne.

She tapped on her screen and studied the scrolling text. *Aha.* There was a shortcut for rebooting. She tapped in some commands.

"Darcy, get back in your seat," Burke ordered.

"Hang on—"

A hand gripped her arm. "I want you in the safest part of the plane."

She looked up, her belly clenching. "I'd prefer *not* to crash at all. There!"

Lights flared all over the console and the pilots gasped.

"She did it," one pilot cried.

The two men burst into action, working together in a flurry of movement and shouting orders at each other.

Burke yanked Darcy back to her feet and dragged her down the aisle between the wide seats.

The plane leveled out and she grinned at him. "The phrase you're looking for is 'thank you, Darcy. You're amazing.'"

He stared at her, and she tilted her head back. A muscle ticked in his jaw. Something emanated off him but she couldn't quite put her finger on it.

"Burke—?"

He grabbed her and yanked her forward. She collided with his hard chest—which, yes, was as hard as she'd imagined in her very-secret, late-night fantasies that she'd never admit to anyone.

Then his mouth slammed down on hers.

Oh. *Oh.*

His lips were firm, and the kiss was hard, hot, and commanding. It was exactly what she'd imagined in those fantasies she'd never admit to having.

Sensations shot straight between her legs, red-hot and insistent.

Darcy's tablet slipped from her fingers, hitting the carpeted floor with a thud. She slid her hands into Burke's hair, a hungry sound escaping her throat. He had glorious, silky, brown hair. She kissed him back with everything she had.

Before she knew it, she was half climbing him, grinding her body against his as he kissed her deeply.

Then he jerked his head back. They stared at each other for a beat.

"Thank you, Darcy. You're amazing." He nudged her into her seat.

Which was lucky, because her knees refused to hold her any longer. She dropped down, trying to catch her breath.

Burke rested his hands on the armrests, caging her in.

He leaned down until his face was an inch from hers. "Now buckle in. We'll be landing soon."

She nodded.

"Guess I've found one way to get you to do what I ask."

As he walked back to the cockpit, Darcy reached up and touched her swollen lips. Wow, the day had really taken a detour into crazy land. A part of her was very satisfied to see Burke's normally neat hair was mussed.

She clipped her belt in place and pulled in a shuddering breath. She turned her head and looked out the window, extremely pleased to see that, while the ground looked much closer, they were no longer hurtling directly toward it.

Body still tingling, Darcy decided she was going to settle into Darcy Denial Land. Where there were no bad guys, no plane crashes, and no sexy, annoying FBI agents who kissed like a dream.

DARCY SIPPED her vanilla latte and smiled. Coffee was the nectar of the gods, and she was pretty darn happy that she was alive to drink it.

Her heels clicked on the creamy travertine tiles as she crossed the cavernous lobby. She loved the Dashwood Museum.

With a nod at the security guards, she stepped into the main hall. Glossy, wooden walls gave the place a sense of history and warmth, and marble columns gleamed in the light. The space was, of course, packed with art. She scanned the room, taking in the magnificent paintings, sculptures, and artifacts.

And in the grand lobby, in less than a week, they were holding the opening of a priceless exhibit. The private collection of a Dashwood donor, who had an extensive assortment of amazing and ancient artifacts.

She took another sip of her coffee, savoring the hit of caffeine. Darcy had a few weaknesses: clothes, shoes, expensive computer parts, and caffeine. She made no apologies for any of them.

She remembered in excruciating detail how it felt to be shy and boring. She'd hit her teens and realized she had two amazingly talented, larger-than-life parents and two tough, athletic larger-than-life brothers. She'd been small and liked computers. Her family were a tough act to follow.

But life was too short to spend apologizing for what you loved or shortchanging yourself. She'd learned to embrace herself.

Yesterday, while her plane was hurtling toward the ground, she'd thought she'd never get another latte again. Today, she'd splurged on a huge breakfast and was on her second coffee of the day. Darcy's mindset right now was to enjoy the heck out of everything. When she got back to Denver, she was making a plan to damn well find the love of her life. Less work, more dating.

But that didn't mean she'd forgotten she had a job to do right now.

She was pretty damned motivated to ensure Silk Road went down. In fiery flames, just like they'd tried to do to her.

The big, opening-gala night would be a who's who of Washington's elite. And the jewels that would lure Silk Road and its mysterious leader, the Collector, would be on display. Energy zinged through her. They were the perfect bait.

Three cursed diamonds.

But first, she needed to finish her work.

She lifted her tablet, studying the security feed. Then she glanced up, taking in the locations of the hidden cameras on the ceiling. She needed to make a few adjustments. Glancing at the screen again, she noted all the angles and blind spots. Thankfully, at this time of the morning, there weren't too many museum-goers. Most people were rushing off to work, and the tourists were still waking up and slowly starting their day.

A deep rumble of a voice echoed from the lobby and Darcy's belly clenched. She knew that voice.

It had been in her dreams last night.

She was still trying to stay in Darcy Denial Land, but the man made it damn difficult. After the plane incident yesterday, Burke had been busy sorting things out with the powers that be. After they'd landed in DC, he'd ordered her to take the day off. Her nose wrinkled. He didn't ask or suggest, no, just a flat-out order. Sometimes she wondered if the man was half machine.

Anyway, Darcy had decided to go shopping. She'd splurged on a bunch of gorgeous lingerie she didn't need but loved. It hadn't quite been the relaxing experience she'd wanted, since she'd been tailed the entire time by an FBI agent escort. One that she *hadn't* been informed about beforehand.

She peeked around the doorway and spotted Burke's back. Another dark suit covered that powerful, muscled body. Instantly, all she could think about was that curl-your-toes kiss.

No. Darcy swiveled back. She wasn't going there. Nopity-nope. The man might kiss like a sex god, but he drove her insane.

Besides, it was clear Alastair Burke lived and breathed his job. Being an FBI agent was in his veins. She'd seen his single-minded focus about taking down Silk Road. In fact, she'd never met a more intense, driven man.

He was far too controlled to fall in love, and he wasn't the kind of man who'd make a woman the center of his world.

Get your work done, Darce. She looked back at the cameras, trying to put firm lips and hard kisses out of her head. She felt someone watching her and looked up.

A businessman stood nearby, studying her with an appreciative look on his face. He was probably a few years younger than her, with a handsome face, blond hair, and a well-cut suit. When he noticed her looking at him, he smiled and nodded.

Hmm, not bad. She smiled back.

Beyond Mr. Cute was a woman with two bored-looking kids in tow. She was attempting to get them interested in a painting by Rembrandt.

Then, loud laughter echoed through the hall. She looked over and saw two young men. They were younger than the businessman—college age, good-looking, and well aware of it. They had thick, over-styled hair, and wore trendy jeans and polo shirts.

The pair were pretending not to look at a pretty sculpture resting on a pedestal. The bronze was of an elegant, naked woman with her back arched, hair flowing down. Darcy looked back at her tablet, and juggling her latte, she swiped the controls. She pulled up the correct camera feed and zoomed in on the young men.

They had trouble written all over them.

She looked up at them again and one caught her eye. A lock of sandy-brown hair fell over his blue eyes and he took his time looking Darcy up and down. He shot her a wide grin. Darcy barely managed to stop her eye roll.

The man-boy sauntered over. "Hi, there."

"Hi." He was lucky to be twenty, and looked spoiled and soft. "Enjoying the museum?"

He gave her fitted jeans and blush-pink sweater a long look, lingering on her breasts. "Oh, yeah."

Puh-lease. "You're an art lover, then?"

"I love beautiful things," he drawled.

God, the guy needed to put some effort into his lines. She saw Mr. Suave's friend edging closer to the sculpture.

"Did you hear about the big exhibit that's coming?" Mr. Suave asked.

"I did hear that somewhere."

He leaned closer. "I heard everyone's busy preparing for the exhibit of the cursed diamonds."

"I heard that, too." A small alert popped up on her tablet, informing her that someone had activated a jammer to block the camera feed. A bad one. She tapped the screen and deactivated it.

"Are you a student?" Mr. Suave nodded at her tablet.

"Well, I am taking notes." She'd already taken snaps of both the man-boys' faces and was running them through the museum's facial recognition system. Anyone who entered the museum and purchased a ticket ended up in the system.

Suave lowered his voice. "You know you're gorgeous?"

Now, Darcy laughed. "Do any of these lines actually work for you, sweetie?"

He blinked and then looked affronted. "All the time."

"On pretty coeds who don't know any better yet."

Suave scowled. "I'm a catch, babe."

"Uh-huh."

That's when his friend nabbed the sculpture off the pedestal. An alarm blared, and instantly, gates descended, shutting off the exits. Both men froze, looking shocked.

The woman cried out, pulled her kids close. The businessman watched with a frown.

"I deactivated your jammer," Darcy told Suave. "You probably weren't aware of all the new security upgrades we've installed." She looked at the tablet and saw that she'd gotten pings on the facial recognition system. "You should have done better research, Patrick."

Mr. Suave sucked in a breath. "How...? They said..."

"Pat!" His friend stood there, still clutching the sculpture.

"It's best if you put that down, James." Darcy tapped, opening the security gate leading from the lobby. "You're about to be arrested."

Patrick straightened, swiping a hand through his floppy hair. His chin jutted forward. "My parents' lawyers will have me out of here in a flash. You have no idea who I am."

Darcy shook her head and tilted her tablet. She showed them the pictures of James snatching the sculpture.

"I caught it all on camera." She cocked her head. "This picture isn't your best angle, Patrick, but it'll still make an impact on Instagram."

"Bitch!"

Patrick lunged. Darcy sidestepped him and stuck out her foot. He tripped over it and fell flat on his face. She pressed her spiked heel into his lower back.

But then James rushed at her to defend his friend. She tensed. *Shit.*

There was a blur, and Burke grabbed James, spun him, and slammed him into a column. The man-boy yelped. Burke cuffed him in about two seconds flat.

Patrick bounced back up and Darcy staggered back. She was pretty sure he had an imprint of her heel in his back now. The man-boy took a few stumbling steps backward.

But Burke was already moving. He grabbed the young man by the neck and shoved him to his knees.

"Hey," Patrick complained.

Burke pulled out another set of cuffs and slapped them on Mr. No-Longer-So-Suave. Burke's face was set in impassive lines and he didn't even look like he'd worked up a sweat.

Damn Alastair Burke for looking so hot. Darcy tried to tame her haywire hormones.

"Gentlemen, this is Special Agent Burke." She sipped her latte again. "He's in charge of the FBI's specialized Art Crime Team." She leaned closer to the young men. "He *really* dislikes people who steal art and antiquities."

Burke looked at her, and although his face was its usual mask, he gave her a little shake of his head. She was pretty sure he was amused.

"They said there'd be no security," Patrick whispered. "That everyone was too busy with the exhibit."

"Who?" Burke demanded, his tone hard. He dragged Patrick to his feet.

Patrick looked ready to pee his pants.

At that moment, several members of the museum security team arrived. One guard detoured to calm the other museum-goers who were still watching in shock.

"We need to question these idiots," Burke said.

Darcy nodded. She pulled in a breath and his yummy cologne hit her. *Focus, Darcy.* "Okay. I already ran these two through facial recognition, and have images of them taking the sculpture. I'll email them to you."

"Darcy." He gave her one of his intense looks. "Good work."

She felt a little flutter in her belly. "Thanks. I have some more work to do on the cameras." She waggled her fingers at the wannabe thieves as she turned.

"Darcy?"

She looked back over her shoulder.

"Don't go too far," Burke said. "Because the diamonds have arrived."

Her pulse leaped. She couldn't *wait* to see the diamonds. Finally, Silk Road, who'd targeted her family, her business, and her friends for years, was going down.

CHAPTER TWO

A lastair Burke liked two things a hell of a lot—order and control.

He especially liked when things were under his control. He shoved the idiot thieves ahead of him into the Dashwood's security room.

One was white-faced but belligerent, and the dark-haired one was crying.

"So, the babe?" Belligerent asked. "She's like museum security?"

Babe? A muscle ticked in Alastair's jaw. "She is none of your concern. You two are in big fucking trouble."

He led them into a small, windowless office. It had a desk and two chairs.

"Sit."

Both boys obeyed.

Alastair's partner, Agent Thomas Singh appeared. The younger man was impeccably dressed, his smile white against his brown skin.

"Busy morning?" The agent handed Alastair a sheaf of papers.

"Looks that way."

"At least there haven't been any crashing planes."

"We aren't joking about plane crashes."

"Right." Thom looked like he was trying not to laugh. "Call me if you need me."

Alastair circled the table and looked at the printouts of Darcy's search. "So, Patrick and James..." he stared at them "...talk."

"It was supposed to be an easy job," Belligerent, also known as Patrick Evan Theodore III said. "No alarms, everybody busy with the new exhibit. Jam the cameras, that's all he said we had to do. He said it'd be a walk in the park."

Alastair's instincts sharpened. "Who?"

"The dude." The other young man—James Frederick Hyland—swiped his cheeks with his sleeve. "He contacted us in a private message in an online group, uh..." He looked nervously at his friend. "A group for people looking for thrills."

God save him from bored, rich kids. "Go on."

The young men were both silent and looked at each other.

Alastair pressed his palms to the table, leaning forward. "If you talk, it might help get a reduction on your charges and possible sentence."

"Sentence?" James squeaked.

"You got caught red-handed trying to steal a valuable artifact from a museum. You can't wriggle out of that."

"Shit." Patrick dropped back in his chair. "Dad's going to kill me."

James' eyes were as wide as dinner plates. "I'm going to Harvard in the fall."

Alastair pushed his jacket back and set his hands on his hips. "Who contacted you?"

"Just a username. Turpan."

The name of an important oasis stopover in China located on the ancient Silk Road route. Alastair bit back a curse. Silk fucking Road. *Dammit.*

There was a knock at the door and Thom poked his head inside. "Police are here."

Both young men moaned.

Alastair stopped by Thom. "Go with them and see if you can get any more information out of them. Silk Road sent them in here for a reason." His partner nodded.

Leaving the security offices, Alastair headed back to the lobby. Workers were setting up display cases for the upcoming exhibit.

And bent over the long, rectangular display where the diamonds would rest was Darcy.

The way she was angled, he had the perfect view of her ass covered by form-fitting dark denim. He stopped, his fingers curling into his palms. He forced himself to take a few deep breaths.

"Darcy."

She swiveled, her glossy, dark hair brushing her jaw. "I was just checking the pressure sensors. How are the man-boys?"

The name made him want to laugh, which was strange, because he never laughed. "On their way to the police station and sweating bullets. Silk Road sent them in here to take the sculpture."

She hissed out a breath. "I'm not surprised." She paused. "For what purpose?"

"Don't know yet. To test the system? To cause problems?" His gaze fell on the display behind her.

The case was currently empty, but soon it would house the three diamonds that would be the centerpiece of the exhibit.

Alastair felt something trickle through him. This was it. This was his chance to finally stop Silk Road once and for all. His gut hardened.

His chance to avenge his mother's murder.

"Burke?"

Darcy was watching him, and he dragged in a breath. His gaze fell to her lips. Today, she'd painted them a soft, sexy pink.

He'd kissed those lips on the plane yesterday, and he'd thought of that kiss every minute of the last twenty-four hours.

She was a pretty big distraction. Burke didn't do distractions.

"Burke?" She was frowning now. "Are you coming down with something?"

"No." He nodded at the case. "Is it ready?"

"Yes. Pressure sensors, cameras." She waved an elegant hand in the air. "The whole place is rigged to the gills."

"Good." He'd known she was the perfect person for this job—smart, clever, and no pushover.

"So, the diamonds are here?" She licked her lips.

Alastair watched her tongue flick out between her soft lips and felt it in his gut. He shook his head. "Yes, they're here. I'll show you."

He moved to take her elbow, when a deep voice echoed across the lobby, followed by heavy footsteps. "Burke!"

Alastair turned and found himself facing one pissed-off brother.

"Declan," Alastair said.

Darcy shot her brother a cautious smile. "Hey, Dec."

Declan Ward crossed his muscular arms over his chest. "You almost got my sister killed yesterday."

The man still looked like the SEAL he'd once been. Starting Treasure Hunter Security with his siblings hadn't softened him one bit. He glared at Alastair with eyes a similar blue-gray shade as his sister's.

"She's fine," Alastair said. "Alive and well."

"She almost ended up in a fucking plane crash."

"Ah, boys—" Darcy started.

They ignored her.

"Silk Road is to blame," Alastair said. "Actually, Darcy was the one who saved the day."

Dec pushed into Alastair's face. "My sister gets hurt, I'm holding you responsible."

Yep, definitely pissed. "I'll make sure that doesn't happen. This just makes it more imperative that our plan to take down the Collector succeeds."

"Hello, I'm in the room." Darcy had crossed her arms, and was tapping the toe of her shoe on the ground.

Dec growled. "She's in Silk Road's sights now, and

you put a target on her. I should never have let her take this job."

Darcy hissed. "Let me? Let me? We're *co-owners* of our business, Declan. You don't give me orders, or pick what jobs I can take."

Burke smiled. He was happy, for once, not to be on the receiving end of Darcy's sharp tongue.

"Darcy—" Dec began.

"No." She sliced her hand through the air. "Silk Road's been targeting you, Cal, and the rest of our team for years. They nearly killed Sloan and Diego just this week. Enough is enough. They need to be stopped."

"It's too dangerous—"

Darcy stepped closer, her killer heels clicking on the tiles, and skewered her brother with a look hot enough to melt metal.

"What? Because I'm female, I can't do my bit? Because I don't have bulging muscles, a gun, or a penis, I can't do my job? Because I'm not a badass ex-SEAL, I can't help protect the people I care about?"

Dec pressed his lips together and thrust his hands on his hips.

Alastair felt a laugh well up in his chest. Damn, that was twice in one day. He cleared his throat.

Two sets of gray eyes swung his way.

"You know, I always wanted a sibling." He paused. "Now I'm kind of glad I'm an only child."

Darcy's eyes, a shade bluer than her brother's, narrowed. Alastair had been around her long enough to know that little move meant she was headed toward blasting him next.

A distraction was required. "Would you like to see the diamonds now?"

Darcy stilled, then turned her back on her brother. "Yes, I would."

Alastair looked at Declan. "I'll do whatever I have to do to ensure her safety."

He saw Darcy's eyes widen, before he moved past her and headed out of the lobby.

DARCY FOLLOWED Burke into the vault, deep in the bowels of the museum. They passed armed guards, and at the heavy-duty metal door, she watched him press his palm to a high-tech lock. The museum had an electronic locking system throughout the building, and Darcy had added several enhancements to it.

The lock beeped and the door opened.

She was still amped up from her argument with Dec. They hadn't shouted...much. Dec could go bossy alpha male at the drop of a hat, but she let him off since she knew he was just worried.

The sooner they had the opening gala and sprung this trap, the better.

Burke stepped back and motioned her into the main vault. The room was lined with shelves, and on a table in the center was a large rectangular box.

Darcy sucked in a breath. Burke waved her closer, and they stood side-by-side in front of the box. He was so close she felt the heat of his body. Butterflies fluttered in her belly. It was just excitement to see the diamonds, of course.

"Ready?" he asked.

She nodded.

He spun the locks on the case and lifted the lid.

She gasped. "Holy cow." Three diamonds were nestled in small impressions in the black velvet.

Two were simply loose stones and one was set in a necklace.

On the left was a huge, blue-tinted, cushion-cut diamond. It was gorgeous.

"That's the Regent," Burke said. "One hundred and forty carats, and considered the most beautiful and purest diamond in the world."

Darcy wouldn't disagree. "Where's it from?"

"It's housed in the Louvre now, and once rested in the crown of Louis XV, adorned the hat of Marie Antoinette, and was set in the pommel of the sword of Napoleon Bonaparte."

"Wow. Quite a pedigree."

"Rumor has it that it came from India. From the Kollur Mine. A slave hid it in an open wound to smuggle it out."

"Ew."

"An English sea captain murdered the slave and stole the diamond. That's how it ended up in Europe." Burke's face remained impassive. "Because so much misfortune fell on those who possessed the stone, it's said to be cursed."

"How much is it worth?"

"About sixty-five million dollars."

Darcy choked. "Holy cow. And the Louvre let you have it?"

"On the proviso that we return it, of course." His tone was dry. He pointed to the diamond on the right. The stone was pear-shaped, smaller in size, and a pale-yellow color.

"That's the Sancy. Fifty-five carats, and also hailing from India, it was once reputed to be owned by the Mughals."

"Who were descended from Mongolian tribes."

"Yes. It's been in and out of the hands of various European royalty. It was brought to Europe by a French soldier, de Sancy. It was rumored to have been carried by a messenger to the king, but he was set upon by thieves. It was thought stolen, but de Sancy was convinced the man was loyal. They cut open the dead man's stomach and found the Sancy inside him."

"Yikes, that's some loyalty." She tilted her head. "What's this one worth?"

"Six and a half million."

Nothing to sneeze at. "And both of these are from the Louvre?"

He nodded. "Once I heard the Black Orlov was a part of the collection going on display at the Dashwood, I knew we needed a little more enticement to ensure the Collector was interested. I convinced the Louvre to add the Regent and Sancy to the exhibit."

Three priceless diamonds...all of them allegedly cursed.

Darcy's gaze fell on the center stone.

This gem was truly unique. It was a dark gray, almost

black against the white diamonds in the necklace framing it.

"The Black Orlov," Burke said. "Almost sixty-eight carats, and also called the Eye of Brahma."

Darcy moved closer. "I read that it's from a shrine in India."

"Yes. Stolen from an ancient statue of the Hindu creator god, Brahma, by a Jesuit monk."

"And it's cursed?"

"It's said to cause whoever possesses it to commit suicide." There was an edge of amusement in his tone. "Rumor says the diamond dealer who first took the Black Orlov to New York to sell it ended up taking his life by jumping off a skyscraper. Later, two Russian princesses who owned it—one named Nadia Orlov, who it was named after—both jumped to their deaths, as well."

Darcy turned to face him. "You don't believe the curse?"

He shrugged. "I don't believe in curses."

"At THS, we've seen some pretty freaky stuff—lost temples, amazing healing salves, certain items confiscated by a mysterious team in black. And I know you have, too."

His green eyes stayed impassive.

"And Team 52—"

"Don't talk about them." Burke turned back to the case. "I have another job for you."

Darcy heaved out a sigh. "Of course, you do. What now?"

"I need trackers placed on each of these diamonds. Trackers that are undetectable."

Her mouth dropped open and she stared at the diamonds. "You're kidding me."

"Nope." Burke crossed his arms. His jacket was unbuttoned, so she had a clear view of the way his white shirt pulled tight on his hard chest.

She tried not to notice, but the guy was ripped, she was sure of it. She'd always imagined FBI agents as a little overweight and balding, but not Burke.

Focus, Darcy. "First of all, tech like that doesn't exist. And to add to the problem, two of these are just loose diamonds. There's nowhere to hide a tracker."

"I know you're up for a challenge."

She growled. "I'm good, Burke, but not a magician."

"So, you're saying you can't do it?"

Damn, she saw the challenge in his eyes. Her brothers had learned early that the quickest way to get her to do something was to challenge her.

It looked like Burke knew her secret. He was manipulating her, dammit. "You think you know me so well."

"I do."

She shook her head.

"I know your middle name," he said.

Her eyes widened. She never told anyone her middle name. "You do not."

"Try me."

She narrowed her gaze. "You repeat it, I'll hack your computer and leave a virus that will make you weep."

The annoying man just raised a brow. "So, the trackers?"

"Fine. I'll see what I can do, but I'm not making any promises."

He looked smug. "Okay."

"If I do this, you owe me. Big time."

His eyes flashed. "Whatever you want. I'll do anything to make sure we catch the Collector."

She heard the iron determination in his voice. Not for the first time, she wondered what drove him. Keeping her tone light, she raised a brow. "Better be careful there, Burke. You have no idea what I might demand."

"I think I can handle it."

Darcy suddenly had the suspicion they were talking about something else. She cleared her throat. "I'll make some calls."

He shot her a faint smile and damn if it wasn't a good one.

Focus, Darcy.

CHAPTER THREE

Alastair stood with his hands on his hips, studying the main lobby. Banners in glossy red had been unfurled from the mezzanine-level railings above, hanging almost to the floor below. They showcased images of the cursed diamonds.

They were another day closer to springing their trap.

"We're nearly ready for the big night." Thom stood beside him, studying the scene as well.

Alastair grunted. He spotted Darcy up on the mezzanine, directing some of the museum security geeks to adjust cameras.

In her dark jeans, knee-high boots, and blood-red sweater, she looked gorgeous. Too damn gorgeous.

Since he'd joined the FBI, he'd let nothing and no one derail his mission. He didn't have time for relationships. Silk Road had killed his mother. They'd hurt her, stolen her life, and destroyed his. From a boy, he'd vowed he wouldn't stop until the organization was dust and his mother had her justice.

"Alastair?"

He looked back at Thom. His partner glanced up at Darcy, then back to Alastair.

"I hope you get your head out of your workaholic ass about that woman."

Alastair was *not* having this discussion. He crossed his arms over his chest.

As usual Thom didn't look fazed. They'd worked together long enough that Thom was immune to the looks and moods that sent younger agents scurrying.

Thom shook his head. "At least tell me you have your tux organized?"

Alastair scowled. "Tux?"

"Yes, a tuxedo, Alastair. For the black-tie opening gala that we've been planning for several weeks."

Alastair ignored the sarcasm. "I'll find something."

Thom, always the fashion plate, held up a hand. "No. I'll arrange it."

"I have something—"

"You have something plain and ill-fitting." Thom ran his gaze over Alastair, like he was sizing him up. "I'll sort it out."

Alastair had more important things to worry about than damn tuxedos. "The agents for the gala have all been briefed."

Thom's face turned serious. "Yes. You picked a good team. Plus, with the Treasure Hunter Security guys backing them up, we'll be well covered."

Alastair had wanted the best. He'd handpicked the best agents and it was the reason he'd brought THS in.

"And the security for the guests—"

Thom nodded. "Guards will be wanding people at the doors. The Dashwood director looked a bit sick when I told him, but he agreed. He has no desire to lose the Louvre's diamonds."

Alastair looked up at the mezzanine again, but Darcy was gone. He frowned. "Where's Darcy?" She'd probably gone to get coffee. Again.

"She mentioned something about going to see someone about the 'fucking impossible trackers Agent Arrogant and Annoying wanted.'" Thom's smile was blinding. "She has you pegged."

Alastair raised a brow. "You want to be reassigned to Alaska, Singh?"

"Ah, no," Thom said. "I don't like the cold."

"You assigned someone to follow Darcy, right? Silk Road is out there, and watching her."

"Of course, I did. Anderson."

Alastair nodded. The agent was good and competent.

Just then, Alastair's phone vibrated and he pulled it out of his pocket. "Burke."

"Sir, it's Agent Anderson."

Burke stiffened. "What's wrong?"

"Miss Ward gave me the slip on New York Avenue NW. I've got no idea where she's headed."

Alastair cursed and snapped his phone shut.

"She gave Anderson the slip."

Thom cursed.

Alastair jogged for the door. "If she comes back, call

me." But Alastair planned to track down the little escape artist himself and give her a piece of his mind.

DARCY STEPPED out of the cab and looked around. Brentwood was not a good area of DC, with a high crime rate, and plenty of worn, ugly apartment buildings.

"Thanks," she said to her driver.

"You sure you want to be here, lady?"

"I'll be fine. Thanks again."

She closed the door and headed up the sidewalk. She kept her chin up and her stride confident. If you seemed like prey, you became prey.

She spotted some young guys eyeing her and she stared back boldly. They remained on their stoop, still watching her, but unmoving.

Avoiding a crack in the sidewalk, she made her way toward a rundown apartment building near the corner. She went to ring the buzzer, but saw that the door lock was busted. Shaking her head, she opened the door and stepped inside. She headed up the stairs. The place was all kinds of grimy, and smelled of smoke, sweat, and urine. Her nose wrinkled. *Nice.*

She quickly made her way to the top floor and knocked on the door she wanted.

A shuffling noise from inside. "Go away."

"Animal, it's Darcy Ward."

There was a pause.

She heard the sound of chains unlocking. The door swung open. Animal was a small, wiry, mixed-race man, with a mop of curly hair that looked like it hadn't been brushed in...maybe a year. His brown eyes were dilated. She knew he had a drug habit, and liked amphetamines—anything that made him go faster and need less sleep.

"Darce." He wiped his hand on his dirty jeans. "I'm busy."

"I told you I was coming." She stepped closer, and when he backed up a step, she pushed inside and shut the door.

There were computers all over the living room. Some were on and working, and others were just disassembled parts. On the main screen, she saw a first-person shooter game going on, and on a smaller screen, she saw Animal was running a hack. On yet another screen, she saw design schematics for...something.

The sagging couch was covered in discarded food wrappers and empty cups. *Gross.*

"Take a seat." He pushed a stack of magazines off a stool and they crashed to the floor.

"I'm fine, thanks." And after this, she was going to douse herself in antiseptic solution.

"Do you want a...?" Looking confused, he glanced toward the kitchen. "Drink?"

She followed his gaze. The small kitchen was filled with filthy dishes. *Hell, no.* "I'm good, thanks."

"So, long time no see, Darce." He slipped his hands into his pockets, causing his baggy jeans to slide lower.

"It's been a while," she said. "I brought you a challenge."

Animal's eyes sharpened. "Oh yeah?"

"I need an undetectable tracker with a decent range."

Animal's brown eyes turned considering. "Might have something. It's best if you can hide it inside—"

She shook her head. "It needs to go on the outside and not be visible. At all."

"Darcy—"

"I need to put the tracker on gemstones."

Animal looked at her for a beat, then threw his head back and laughed hysterically. "Not possible."

"It needs to be small, obviously. Transparent—"

He shook his head. "Nope."

"Come on, Animal. I know you get your hands on a lot of stuff." Military-grade, experimental stuff. She had no idea how he did it, or who gave it to him. And she didn't ask.

His eyes flickered. "Nope. Don't have anything like that."

"Come on. I'll pay."

"Pay?"

"Whatever you want."

He looked tempted for a beat, then shook his head.

"I'll get you gear." She knew his weakness. "Something top-of-the-line." Darcy wracked her brain and a thought hit her. "How about a drone? Best you've ever seen."

Animal went still. "A drone? I like drones."

"It may not be working, but I can at least get you some parts." She pulled up her tablet and accessed her private server. She pulled up a recording that showed the high-tech drone that the mysterious Team 52 had used in Africa when they'd collided with THS on a mission.

Animal's gaze locked on the screen and turned hungry. He licked his lips. "I want it."

She smiled and turned the video off. "You make me three small trackers that can't be detected, and I'll get you the drone parts."

His eyelids twitched. "It'll take time to put them together..."

"I need them in two days."

"Darce," he groaned. "You're killing me."

"Do we have a deal?" She wasn't risking shaking hands. She didn't want to pick up something infectious.

Animal sighed. "Deal. Sometimes I regret meeting you in the gaming chat room years ago."

She winked at him. "No, you don't."

Suddenly, there was a thud at the door. They both turned, just as the door flew open and two guys with guns raced in. They were covered in tattoos and wearing baggy jeans.

Uh-oh. Gang members.

Animal spun to face the men. "Oh, hey, Spider. King."

"You owe us money, Animal," the one with a shaved head said. He had the tattoo of a large spider on the side of his neck.

The other one was taller and broader, with dark hair and a tight, white T-shirt. His gaze fell on Darcy and lit up. "Who's the classy piece?"

Animal's face turned green. "King, she's—"

"Hi, I'm Darcy," she said. "I was just leaving."

She took one step, but the dark-haired man, King, sidestepped and blocked her.

Double uh-oh.

"Help! Help!" Animal screamed.

Both men lifted their handguns. One fired. Bullets hit the wall above her head and Darcy ducked. Animal dived to the side and careened into a table of junk. It collapsed under his weight.

King moved toward Darcy, arm outstretched.

She grabbed it, bent her knees and shifted her weight. She threw him over her shoulder. He landed flat on his back on the dirty carpet, blinking at the ceiling.

"My brothers are both former Navy SEALs. They taught me self-defense. And my mother's no slouch in a fight, either."

Spider was still standing and lifted his gun, aiming at her face. "Oh, yeah? Got any fancy moves that can beat a bullet?"

Darcy froze. *Shit.*

Then she saw movement in the doorway. Burke strode through the door and her heart leaped.

His suit jacket flared out behind him and his face was grim.

He came up behind Spider and landed a hard chop to the gangbanger's neck. The man cried out, his gun falling to the dirty carpet. Spider spun, only to meet a hard punch to the face. The thug stumbled backward, and Burke gripped the guy, spun him, and slammed him face first into the wall.

Burke pulled cuffs off his belt.

Wow. The man did not mess around.

Darcy saw movement out of the corner of her eye. King leaped to his feet and charged at Burke.

Burke's face didn't change, just stayed cool and collected. He kicked at King's arm. The gun went off, a bullet hitting the ceiling, then the gun spun and fell somewhere near the couch. Burke followed through with a hard jab, then a mean hook. King made a pained sound. Burke stepped closer, rammed a punch into the man's gut, then elbowed him in the face.

There was an ugly crunch that made Darcy wince, and then King went to his knees, gurgling.

Burke dragged King over by his buddy and handcuffed him as well.

Animal got back to his feet, looking freaked.

Burke pointed a finger at Darcy. "You and I are going to have a discussion."

She crossed her arms. "I had it under control." Okay, she hadn't, but she knew "discussion" meant a whole lot of yelling and orders.

He strode up to her until he was only an inch away. "You had a gun in your face."

Right, not so great. "Burke—"

He grabbed her arm. "You do not give your escort the slip."

"I didn't need company. Animal is—" twitchy, does highly illegal stuff "—sensitive."

Animal made a choked sound and turned to Darcy. "You brought *Superman* with you?"

"Not Superman, just Special Agent Very Arrogant and Annoying."

Burke's green eyes flashed. She was pretty sure he wanted to either shake her or choke her.

"Special Agent," Animal squeaked.

"FBI," Burke growled, scanning the apartment.

"He's not here for you." Darcy stepped away from Burke. "Animal is going to get us trackers."

"I can get you the hardware," Animal said. "But the programming—"

"I can take care of that," Darcy said.

"Go." He waved them off. "If anyone sees I have the FB-fucking-I in my place, I'll be screwed."

"I have police coming to pick up these two," Burke said.

Animal squeaked again, his eyes going wide. "The *police.*" His eyes rolled around wildly.

"We'll pull them out into the hall," Darcy said.

From beside her, Burke growled.

"Thanks, Animal," Darcy said cheerily.

He just glared at her.

Muscle ticking in his jaw, Burke snatched up the handguns lying on the carpet, then dragged the two groaning gang members onto the landing. Darcy followed, and as soon as they were out, Animal slammed the door shut. Moments later, two uniformed officers came up the stairs.

"Agent Burke?" one officer said.

"Yeah. I have two gang members for you. Both threatened Ms. Ward here and discharged weapons." Burke handed over the handguns.

The officer eyed the two handcuffed men. "Hey, Spider. Hey, King." He looked at Burke. "We'll take it from here."

With a nod, Burke gripped Darcy's arm and yanked her down the stairs.

"Burke—"

"Be quiet."

"Really, I—"

"You're a trouble magnet."

She made a scoffing sound. "Excuse me—"

With a swift move, Burke backed her into the wall. She looked into his face and gasped. All that usual rock-solid control was crumbling.

"Do. Not. Sneak. Out. Again." His voice was clipped and seething.

"Don't give me orders, Alastair."

"You need them."

"Excuse me? I have a perfectly good brain—"

He leaned closer, his nose brushing hers. "You need to be quiet." Something moved through his eyes. "On the plane, I discovered one way to shut you up and keep you out of trouble."

Her heart hammered in her chest, and it wasn't from fear. She licked her lips and his gaze dropped to her mouth

"Really, you are so arrogant—"

His mouth crashed down on hers. Fueled by anger and other emotions, his tongue speared into her mouth. She moaned, sliding hers along his. She pressed into him and the kiss was deep and fierce.

Then he pulled back, his face unreadable. Darcy tried to get her brain cells working again, but they'd decided to take a vacation.

Then Burke took her hand and pulled her out the door.

CHAPTER FOUR

O nce parked in front of the Dashwood Museum, Alastair got out of his car and stormed around to the passenger side. Darcy was already out of the car, and he grabbed her hand, tugging her along. He heard her heels clicking on the sidewalk.

"Burke, quit dragging me around like a dog," she snapped.

He ignored her and headed up the wide, marble steps, past the elegant columns, and into the museum.

As soon as they were inside, the tightness in his chest eased. She was safe. He could breathe again.

On the drive back to the museum, all he'd kept seeing in his head was the image of Darcy in that shitty apartment, with a gun pointed at her head.

He spun to face her. "You need to learn to follow orders."

"I'm neither a soldier nor a robot." Her chin lifted. "You need to act less like a dictator and more like a person. Make the odd request, use your manners, have a feeling or two."

"I feel."

"Really? Most of the time, you don't show a flicker of emotion."

He was feeling a whole chaotic mess of emotions right now, with fury leading them all. He sucked in a breath.

"You're just so driven," she muttered. "Sometimes I don't think you care about anything except taking down Silk Road."

For years, that had been all he'd cared about. All he should care about. "Think you can stay out of trouble for longer than a few minutes?"

She crossed her arms, and he tried not to look at the way it pushed her breasts up against the tempting red fabric of her sweater.

"No," she said.

"Darcy—" His voice was little more than a growl.

"You wanted trackers, I got them."

"I want you *safe*." The last word was close to a yell, echoing in the lobby. Damn, the woman worked his nerves.

"I won't be safe until Silk Road is stopped. None of us will be."

He stared at her, knowing she was right. He knew she was willing to risk everything, even her own safety, to take the group down. She wanted to protect her family and friends.

He understood better than anyone. Although he had something else driving him—vengeance.

"Isn't that what you want?" she asked. "To stop them?"

"Not if it costs your life." Shock hit him as the words tumbled out.

Her eyes widened.

Thom appeared and cleared his throat. "Children, everyone in the museum can hear you arguing."

Darcy swiveled. "Thom, I need caffeine."

Thom shook his head and smiled. "I'll get you a latte, Darcy."

She tossed the man a wide smile. She always had a smile for his partner.

"Chai, please."

"Sure."

"Extra shot." She pulled a face. "I wouldn't say no to a shot of whisky." She glanced at Alastair. "I might need it for courage."

Alastair narrowed his gaze on her. "Why?"

"I have something else to tell you."

He set his hand on a hip and looked at his shoes. They were scuffed from the scuffle with Spider and King, and Alastair liked them shiny. He pulled in a deep breath, wondering what in the hell she could possibly say next to drive him out of his mind.

"Tell me."

"I promised Animal payment for the trackers."

Alastair sighed. "How much?"

"He doesn't want money."

Alastair felt a prickle on his neck. He always got it before something bad happened. "I'm not going to like this, am I?"

She shot him a hesitant smile. "I need you to put me in touch with Team 52."

He sucked in a breath. "No."

"Yes. He wants a look at their fancy drone. That's what Animal gets off on, pulling bits of advanced tech apart."

"These are not people you want to notice you, Darcy."

"You said they were the good guys."

"They're a covert black ops team. They do *anything* to achieve their objectives, no matter what. They are not going to willingly hand over their experimental tech to a drug-addicted hacker."

"Animal is harmless." She cocked a hip. "I'm pretty sure Team 52 has as many reasons as we do to help take Silk Road down."

Alastair heaved out a breath. "Tell your friend we'll pay him in cash."

"He won't take it. Tech is what floats his boat."

"Darcy."

"Look, if you want trackers, you've got to give him something. It can just be parts. It doesn't have to be operational."

Alastair pressed a hand to the back of his neck. "I'll see what I can do."

She clapped her hands together. "Thank you." She tilted her head. "Don't you have a meeting at FBI Headquarters soon?"

His gaze narrowed. "How the hell do you know that?"

She blinked. "You must have mentioned it?"

"I didn't." He scowled at her. "Tell me you haven't been hacking my computer again."

"Who me?"

He growled and looked at his partner. "I'll be at Headquarters. I have a meeting, and now I also need to make a call." He speared Darcy with a look. "Stay inside the museum, don't hack the FBI, and stay out of trouble."

She pulled a face.

"Please."

Her eyes warmed and the corner of her mouth quirked. "I promise, staying out of trouble is my middle name."

Thom made a strangled sound that was clearly a poorly hidden laugh.

"No, your middle name is Aphrodite. Darcy Aphrodite Ward."

Her mouth formed an O. "I promised retribution if you ever spoke that aloud."

"I think it's pretty, and Thom won't tell." Alastair looked at his partner. "Look after her."

Thom nodded. "On it."

"After you get me a latte," Darcy added.

With one last look at Darcy, Alastair strode out. Damn, she turned him inside out. He headed down the steps toward his car.

All his life, he'd been dedicated to taking Silk Road down. He'd helped form the Art Crime Team to focus on the crimes Silk Road committed. He'd spent his career gathering data on the syndicate and the people who ran it. He'd promised his mother's memory that he'd do *everything* to make them pay, whatever the cost.

But now, one woman's life was more important than his mission.

Alastair paused at the bottom of the steps. He thought of his mom—sweet and smiling. Then he thought of those terrifying moments, when he'd been locked up, trapped, listening to his mother's screams. He'd been helpless.

His jaw clenched so hard it hurt. He made his way to his car and settled behind the wheel. He was taking Silk Road down, and he was personally going to ensure Darcy Ward stayed alive. But he had to quit letting her get to him, and he really needed to stop kissing her.

He was going to keep some distance between them and focus on his job.

Back at FBI Headquarters, he walked through the offices, listening to the familiar sounds of his colleagues going about their business. Staff bustled around, telephones rang. Some agents were escorting people in for questioning.

He attended his meeting and updated his boss. Then he locked himself in his office and pulled his laptop closer. He tapped the keyboard and put through a video call.

A tattooed man appeared, the dark frames of his glasses dominating his face. "Hello, Agent Burke. Please stand by."

"Thanks, Brooks."

The image changed, and a tough, rugged face filled the screen. Stubble covered the man's hard jaw, and he looked back at Alastair with cool, golden eyes.

Scary, assessing eyes.

"Burke," the man said.

"Hunter." The leader of Team 52 looked as tough as he always did. "I've heard some pretty wild reports coming out of Las Vegas recently."

Team 52 was based outside of Las Vegas. Most of their work was classified, but Alastair had crossed paths with them a few times before. The covert team was tasked with containing and safeguarding certain objects and artifacts. Ancient technology that had certain abilities—dangerous ones.

Alastair had been shocked to learn that conventional history lessons didn't quite have their facts correct, and that advanced human civilizations had once existed long, long ago. Those civilizations had been wiped out by the rising floodwaters at the end of the last ice age. Sometimes, artifacts from those cultures emerged. Artifacts with abilities they didn't quite understand, and that bad people—like Silk Road—fought to get their hands on.

Recently, Alastair had heard of several incidents in Las Vegas. He knew it had something to do with an artifact that had been stolen, and Team 52 had been tasked with recovering it.

Hunter didn't reply for a moment, but his lips twitched. "It was pretty wild."

Alastair stared in surprise. Hunter wasn't a man who smiled. Ever. Alastair studied the man more closely. He looked his usual, tough self, but there was something... more relaxed about him.

"What can I do for you, Burke?"

"You know I'm laying a trap for Silk Road?"

The man nodded. "With cursed diamonds. Good bait."

"I need trackers to put on the diamonds."

Hunter opened his mouth, but Alastair held up a hand. "I already have them, an...ally is making them for us. An eccentric inventor."

"Civilian?"

Alastair thought of Animal. "Yes. In return, he wants some advanced tech to study. He's heard about your drone."

Hunter's face darkened.

"Doesn't have to be operational, Hunter. Just a few parts."

"You can't be serious?"

"Help us bring down Silk Road, once and for all. It'll make all our jobs easier and the world a little safer."

Hunter released a long breath.

"I want Silk Road finished," Alastair added. "They're targeting the people working with me. People I want to keep safe."

Golden eyes flashed. "A woman?"

Alastair didn't respond, just held Hunter's stare.

Apparently, Hunter didn't need a verbal answer. "Damn their pretty, smart hides. They can make you do things you never believed you'd do."

Alastair blinked. Hell, Hunter had a woman?

"Fine," the man said. "I'll have Brooks courier some parts to you. Not much, and nothing sensitive. I'll already have to go to war with our grumpy tech guru. He won't be happy to part with a single bolt. Not to mention my boss."

Alastair nodded. "Appreciated. I owe you."

Hunter nodded. "You do, and one day I'll cash in. Take care of your woman, Burke." The screen went blank.

Suddenly, there was a hammering on Alastair's office door. A junior agent entered, panic on his face.

Alastair leaped to his feet. "What is it?"

"Problem at the Dashwood, sir. Alarms are going off—"

In three strides, Alastair grabbed a fistful of the man's shirt. "Tell me."

"Some sort of chemical attack. Right in the main lobby."

Right where he'd left Darcy working.

Alastair ran out of the room. Silk Road had gone too far this time.

Darcy. He had to get to her.

DARCY STAGGERED through the white cloud fogging the room, coughing. Her eyes were burning, tears streaming down her face. Her chest was in agony and she wheezed, trying to work air in and out of her lungs.

Moans and cries echoed around her. Other people were trying to escape the gas. Her vision was blurry, and she wasn't even sure if she was heading for the door. She'd been working on the display and everything had been fine. Then she'd smelled the sharp scent of bleach.

Her toe nudged something. No, *someone*. "You have

to get up." She could see the cloud was thicker near the floor.

She tugged on the person, hearing them coughing violently. Darcy got the woman on her feet, and they staggered forward together.

The burning in Darcy's chest was growing worse. A coughing fit hit her, and the woman she was helping pulled away. Darcy tried to draw in air, but it hurt too much. She collapsed to the floor.

God, after this job, she was going to the beach. She wanted a nice vacation villa by the sand, a plunge pool, and no bad guys. Her hazy mind turned over, wondering what Alastair would look like shirtless, rising out of a pool.

She coughed again and she swallowed a cry of pain. She couldn't breathe.

Then she saw figures looming in the smoke ahead. Giant shapes. Her heart clenched in her chest in a moment of panic.

Darcy's vision cleared for a split second, and she realized that it was people in hazmat suits. They were trying to help the people collapsed on the floor.

She lifted a hand, trying to call for help. But no one spotted her and she curled up in a ball. Everything ached and she couldn't breathe anymore.

Then, strong arms slid under her and lifted her up. She looked into Alastair's face. He wasn't wearing a hazmat suit, but he had a mask on.

"I've got you." His voice was muffled. He pulled her close to his chest and strode through the lobby.

"Alastair—" She broke into another coughing fit.

"Don't talk." He headed outside, jogging down the stairs.

"I just...survived an attack...and you're still bossy." But she rested her head on his shoulder.

"And still talking. Quiet, Darcy."

"Thanks...for coming to get me."

With a shake of his head, he made a beeline for one of the ambulances waiting outside. There were people everywhere—cops, agents, paramedics, firefighters. They passed Thom who was sitting with a paramedic, an oxygen mask over his face, his hair disheveled.

Burke set her down on a gurney. "Check her over."

A male paramedic spun into view.

"Now," Burke ordered.

The paramedic hovered over her, pressing an oxygen mask over her mouth. He started checking her vitals.

Burke went to step away, but Darcy grabbed his hand and squeezed it tight. His fingers laced with hers and he moved closer.

"What...happened?" She winced at the ache in her raw throat.

"Chlorine gas attack. I got word on the way over here."

"Fucking Silk Road." She coughed again.

"Try not to talk," the paramedic said.

"She's not very good at that," Burke muttered.

Over her mask, Darcy tried to glare at him, but she started coughing again, ruining the effect.

"Chlorine is a common chemical," Burke said. "It's easy for someone to get their hands on it, then sneak a device into the museum. We're looking for it now." His fingers stroked her hand.

"You're fine." The paramedic stepped back. "Now that you're no longer exposed, your symptoms will fade, and you'll start to feel better. You weren't exposed long enough to have any long-lasting effects, but get yourself checked by your doctor."

Darcy saw Burke let out a big breath. He nodded at the paramedic. "Thanks." Then he touched her hair, sliding it behind her ear.

The concern she saw in his green eyes made her tremble.

"You just can't stay out of trouble," he said.

"This is hardly my fault."

"What the fuck?" An angry male voice.

"Uh-oh," she murmured behind her mask. "Incoming."

Dec appeared, his face thunderous. He leaned down and pulled her into a hard hug. "Thank God." He exhaled loudly. "You're going back to Denver."

"No." She scowled at him.

Burke's face hardened. "I agree with Declan."

Darcy looked up at him, shock spilling through her. "What? No. I'm seeing this through."

"Silk Road is stepping up their attacks," Burke said. "They know we're planning something, and that you're integral to that plan."

"All the more reason I help finish this," she said.

"The Collector won't be deterred." Burke's face was set in stark lines. "And he might kill you in the process."

Dec spun to face Burke. "You promised to protect her."

Burke straightened. "I won't let her get hurt again. I'm not leaving her side."

"Hello? Adult woman here, you macho neanderthals."

Both men swiveled their heads, pinning her with hard stares. Luckily, Darcy had lots of practice dealing with alpha males.

"I'm finishing this," she said.

Both their scowls deepened.

She tore the mask off. "So, both of you stand beside me and help me. Don't get in my way, or try and take me out of the game."

They glared at her and she lifted her chin.

"Shit," Dec muttered. "I know that look. She's not going to give in."

"She will if I handcuff her and drag her onto a plane," Burke said.

She narrowed her gaze. "Try it."

"Don't tempt me." They glared at each other for a few more seconds, then Burke gave a jerky nod. "I'm with you every second of the day until this is done."

Butterflies winged through her belly. Hmm, that was going to be interesting. "Can we get back to work now?" she said. "About the trackers..."

"I got what you need," Burke said.

Her eyes widened. "You did? That's great. I could kiss you."

The vibe between them changed and she watched his gaze drop to her lips.

No. Fight it. Darcy felt tingles in places she didn't want to feel, especially not with her brother watching. And Dec rarely missed a thing. His eyes narrowed as he studied them both.

An agent called for Burke and he held up a hand. He looked at Dec. "You'll stay with her until I take care of this."

Dec lifted his chin and they both watched Burke stride off. Someone handed him an earpiece and he slid it into his ear. He was mobbed by people.

"We have to finish this, Dec." Darcy watched the chaos all around them. All caused by Silk Road. Her gaze fell on a disheveled woman coughing against a paramedic.

Dec released a breath and nodded. "I know."

"I want everyone safe. And you have Layne to think about now too."

"Yeah."

"She must be missing you."

A smile curled her brother's lips at the mention of his wife. "I'm missing her too. But the time away means we're both very eager to see each other."

Darcy raised a palm. "Ew, please." But she smiled. "I'm so happy for you, Dec. She loves you so much, and you look at her the same way Dad looks at Mom." Darcy let out a gusty sigh.

Dec gripped her shoulder. "You'll find the right guy, Darce. And if he treats you wrong, I'll shoot him."

She bumped her shoulder against his side. "I've never been in love. Attraction, sure—"

Dec stiffened. "Stop right there. There are things a brother doesn't want to hear. Ever."

She laughed and then her gaze zeroed in on Alastair. No surprise, he looked like he was issuing orders.

"About you and Burke—" Dec started.

"There is no me and Burke."

"You're a smart woman, Darcy."

She waved a hand, trying to keep her tone light. "He's married to his job, Dec. I want...I want more than to be second best and accepting scraps." She'd dated guys where she'd fallen far down their priority list. "I want a guy who sweeps me off my feet, who puts me first. I want the damn fairy tale."

Dec frowned. "You deserve someone who loves you. But love isn't always a fairy tale, Darce. There are good days and bad days, arguments and laughter, give and take. Loving someone, and wanting them safe and happy, takes effort, but love makes it all worthwhile."

She made a humming sound.

"If you think Mom and Dad don't fight and want to kill each other sometimes, then you're wrong."

Darcy saw Alastair heading back. His face was focused and she knew he was running through a dozen things in his head. For now, they had a job to do. That's what they all needed to be focused on.

She ran her hands through her hair, tidying it. "Can you guys clear the museum, so I can get back to work?"

Dec put his hands on his hips and looked at the sky.

"You're not going back to work today," Burke said.

She blinked. "What?"

"You were just exposed to a chemical. You're going back to your hotel to rest."

"Excuse me, no." Darcy swung her legs off the gurney and stood.

Dec was still watching, but with amusement now. "For once, I agree with him."

"You, be quiet," she said.

"You're resting," Burke ordered.

"N-O. It spells a word that means I'm not following your orders."

His face changed, darkening. Then he set his hands on Darcy's waist. She gasped at the touch. Then he lifted her, and she found herself tossed over a broad shoulder.

Speechless, all she could do was hang there. He did *not* just do that.

"Put me down!"

"No." He stalked toward his car.

"Burke!" She lifted her head and saw everyone was watching them.

"No."

"You are so *annoying*."

She found herself lowered into the passenger seat of his car. She crossed her arms over her chest and stared out the window.

Arrogant, annoying asshole.

CHAPTER FIVE

"I'm fine."

Alastair ignored Darcy's assurance as he followed her into the lobby of her hotel.

He felt unsettled, adrenaline still circulating in his system. He'd been so fucking afraid. The mad drive from FBI headquarters to the Dashwood had felt like it'd taken a hundred years.

And every mile of the way, his head had been filled with images of Darcy dead. Gone. He'd sprinted up the steps and burst through the agents who'd tried to hold him back, fighting to get inside and get to her.

Before, vengeance for his mother had fueled him.

Now, Silk Road had no idea of just what they'd ignited in him.

Darcy jabbed the up button on the elevator. "I can get myself to my room, Burke. Better yet, I can go back to work."

The doors opened and he nudged her inside.

She spun, attitude radiating off her. "Don't you think I've forgotten your caveman tactics back at the museum, either—" Her words cut off with a gasp.

Alastair watched her face go pale and she started to wilt. He lunged, wrapping an arm around her and catching her before she fell.

"You were saying?" he muttered.

"I'm...I'm a little dizzy."

He cursed under his breath and lifted her into his arms. The doors opened and he moved down the hall. "You need to start listening to me."

"I might if you quit with the orders. How about asking, discussing, using some manners?"

"I'm used to giving orders."

She snorted. "No kidding."

"I'm...not good with niceties." One, he was out of practice, and two, they took time. He preferred to get the job done as fast as possible.

"You're a smart man, Burke." Dark brows arched over blue-gray eyes. "I'm pretty sure you can work it out. Practice makes perfect."

They reached her door and he studied her face. Her color was better. He set her down close to the wall and took the keycard from her hand.

She snatched it back. "Remember two seconds ago? We talked about asking?"

He heaved out a breath, then waved a hand at the electronic lock.

She inserted the card and opened the door.

She'd taken two steps inside, when he heard glass

crunch under her heels. He wrapped an arm around her belly and pulled her back against him.

"Oh no!" she cried.

The room was trashed. Furniture had been toppled, the bed was torn up, and her clothes were strewn everywhere.

"Fucking fuck," she spat.

Alastair pulled his Glock, and pushed Darcy back toward the door. "Stay here." He paused. "Please."

She pulled her gaze off her ruined things and looked at him. Her lips quirked. "Since you asked so nicely."

He quickly cleared the room. There was no one here now.

He came back to her, eyeing a scrap of black lace resting on an overturned chair. Darcy gasped and snatched up the tiny panties.

"Don't touch anything," he said. "I'll call it in. They'll want to dust for prints."

"My things...?"

"Once the police clear the place, I'll get them to you." He yanked out his phone and made a call to hotel reception. "This is Special Agent Burke, FBI. Put me through to your Security."

Darcy sighed. "We both know who's responsible for this."

He nodded. "Another warning."

She lifted her chin, eyes flashing. "Silk Road can take their warning and shove it."

A voice came on the line. "Hotel Security."

"I'm in Room 531," Alastair said. "There's been a break in. Can you send someone up?" He waited for the response. "Thanks." He ended the call. "There's a chance they came looking to see if there was any data on what we have planned at the Dashwood."

"I didn't have anything here," she said.

He nodded. "Okay, come on." He nudged her out the door.

"I'm sure the hotel can find me another room."

"No. The hotel is compromised."

"Declan is two floors above."

"No."

She frowned up at him. "Then another hotel."

Alastair grabbed her hand. He could already see that her energy was flagging. After the chlorine gas attack, she needed to be in bed, resting. "No. I need you somewhere safe."

She frowned. "Where?"

"A place I know with top-of-the-line security. Where I can keep an eye on you." He met her gaze. "My place."

"What?" she breathed.

"You can stay with me." Alastair wasn't taking any more risks. Not with her life.

Darcy's dark eyebrows shot up. "No. No. *No.*"

"This is one of those times where I'm not asking."

"Burke—"

"It's an order, Darcy."

The elevator dinged and a man in a dark suit exited. "You called Security?"

"Yes." Alastair stepped forward. "There's been a break in—"

The man lunged and Alastair barely managed to dodge. He heard Darcy cry out. There was a crackling sound and that's when Alastair saw the man was holding a stun gun.

Alastair charged forward, dodged again, trying to land a punch. But the man was fast, swinging the stun gun. One touch and Alastair would go down.

Suddenly, Darcy rammed into the man's back, landing a blow to the man's kidney.

He grunted, spun, and pressed the stun gun to her belly.

"No." Alastair rushed toward them. He had to protect her.

Darcy collapsed to the floor.

Alastair felt a sharp pain at his side, felt his knees give way. His body shuddered and his gaze locked on Darcy. Then everything went black.

"DARCE. COME ON, OPEN THOSE EYES."

Darcy wrinkled her nose. Dec's voice was interrupting her nap. She felt her brother's fingers at her wrist. Was he checking her pulse?

She blinked her eyes open. Why was she on the floor in the hotel corridor? She frowned. She saw people in suits everywhere.

She looked up at Dec crouched beside her and everything came swimming back.

The chemical attack. Her trashed room. The man attacking her and Alastair.

"Alastair!" She sat bolt upright.

Thom appeared behind Dec, his face grim. "What happened, Darcy?"

"We got here, my room was trashed. A man came, said he was Security. He attacked us with a stun gun." She looked around. "Where's Alastair? Is he okay?"

Thom pulled in a deep breath. "He's not here."

"What?" she breathed.

"Looks like they took him."

Her stomach did a slow, sickening roll. "His phone?"

"Off or destroyed."

"Security footage—"

"I have people searching it now." Thom looked worried and pissed.

Darcy pulled out her tablet and let Dec help her up. "I want access. Now."

Thom called for hotel security and moments later, she was in their feed. She tapped, running one of her image search programs.

"Come on, come on."

"Darcy, you need to take it easy," Dec said.

"When he's safe." She looked at her brother. "He came for me. Ran right through the chlorine gas to get me out."

Her brother released a breath and nodded. "We'll find him."

Her tablet dinged. "There!"

She tilted the screen. The video showed a quick glimpse of two men carrying a third between them. She knew instantly the limp, suited man was Alastair. He was clearly unconscious, head lolling forward.

Please be okay.

"That was near a service elevator. Seven minutes ago. They know the camera locations and are avoiding them." She tapped again. "They must have a vehicle close by."

Thom nodded. "They can't go far carrying an unconscious man without people noticing or asking questions."

"I'll find their car." Using the location and possible exits, she narrowed it down. "These vehicles left the hotel at the right time frame." The list flashed up.

"Send it to me," Thom said. "We'll run them down."

Bing.

An email notification flashed on Darcy's tablet. Frowning, she clicked on it. What she saw made her suck in a breath.

"Oh, my God."

The others crowded around her. Dec and Thom cursed.

It was a live video showing Alastair slumped in the bottom of what looked like a large box made of clear, thick plastic. He was sitting against one side, chin resting on his chest.

A timer was ticking below the image, showing just less than an hour. Her gut cramped. There was also a message.

The box is sealed and air tight. You have an hour until Agent Burke runs out of air. Leave the diamonds on the loading dock at the back of the Dashwood Museum, and ensure all security cameras are disabled. Tick tock.

Darcy shook her head. "This can't be happening. Damn Silk Road to hell."

Thom swiveled. "Find the car. I need to know where it went and where he is. Now!"

"He can't be far," Darcy said. "They only had about ten or fifteen minutes to get him out and send me this message."

"Let's set up in my room," Dec said.

Soon, Darcy was sitting at the desk in Dec's suite, having shoved all the magazines and the hotel guide on the floor. Trying to make herself calm down, she analyzed the image of Alastair. He was still unconscious.

Panic was an ugly, hard feeling in her chest. "It looks like a warehouse, or basement. Plain concrete walls, empty of anything else." At least in view of the camera trained on Alastair.

"You can run a search on warehouses and basements in the search radius, right?" Dec asked.

Her fingers flew over the screen. "Already doing it." She huffed out a breath. "But there are way too many results."

"Come on, Darcy. Use that amazing brain of yours. There must be a way to narrow it down."

"Okay, okay." She drummed her nails on the desk. Her mind was still sluggish from the gas attack. But Alastair needed her. "Thom, any luck tracing the cars?"

The agent was seated at the coffee table, phone to his ear and a laptop in front of him. "We think it was the silver Cadillac. It was headed north. Got agents pulling street cameras to see if we can find it."

Darcy tapped a finger against her lip. *North.* That could narrow it a little. She restricted the search to all basements, warehouses, and industrial spaces north of the hotel.

A rock lodged in her throat. "Still too many!" She smacked her palm on the desk.

Suddenly, on the screen, Alastair lifted his head.

"He's awake!"

He shifted, studying his plastic prison. He pressed his hands to the plastic, clearly testing it. He pushed with both hands, before ramming a shoulder against it.

It didn't give. Darcy bit her lip.

"Hang on, Alastair," she murmured.

Thom appeared, staring at his partner. The time ticked down ominously.

"Give me your list of locations," the agent said. "I'll send teams to start searching."

She nodded, but she knew it would take too long to search them all. Alastair would run out of air before they finished.

Panic ate at her insides. She'd felt like this before, when the THS team was in the field and under attack. She hated the sense of helplessness.

She kept her gaze on Alastair. He was studying the room now, turning his head.

Darcy froze. He was wearing an earpiece.

If he wasn't too far away...

She tapped fast on the screen. A quick hack into the FBI's system and she had the right comms channel.

"Burke?"

His head snapped up. "—arcy?"

The line was terrible, but she could hear him. "Thank God! We're trying to find you." She had no idea how much he could hear. She sensed the others in the room moving closer.

"...basement...large. Some crates...far wall."

"Okay."

"Something writ...them. Shipping codes... LS, dash, D525."

"Got it. I'm running a search now. You hold on."

She watched her program churning through data and willed it to go faster. Every second felt like a minute. When she looked back at Alastair, she saw him drag in a deep breath. Her pulse tripped. There was still time on the clock, not much, but he was already feeling the effects.

"Getting...der to breathe," Alastair said.

"Stay calm. Breathe slowly." She pressed a fist to her chest. "We're going to get you out."

"Darcy—"

"Quiet."

He slumped against the side of the box and pressed a hand to the plastic. "You stop them. No...ter what."

"Damn you, quit talking." She touched her screen. "We're stopping them together."

His face looked calm as he looked up, right at the camera. "I wish—"

Beep.

She sat up. The search on the shipping code had found something.

"I've got something. Langsdale Shipping." She sucked in a breath. "He's at the Dashwood. They put him in a basement at the Dashwood."

Darcy was aware of a flurry of activity behind her. She leaped to her feet and looked at her screen. "Hold on, Alastair, we're coming to get you."

CHAPTER SIX

His eyelids felt like they weighed a ton and a bead of sweat rolled down his temple. Alastair let his head drop forward and pulled in another long, shuddering breath.

That's when he heard doors slam open and the sound of running footsteps. Cavalry was here.

People swarmed around his plastic prison and Thom's face appeared beside him.

"Hang on, Alastair."

Then he saw Darcy.

She shouldered through the crowd, still wearing her ice-pick heels, although her usually neat swing of hair was mussed. They'd had a hell of a day, but she still looked beautiful.

Thom was issuing orders. "Get that saw in here and cut this open. Move it."

Darcy's eyes were filled with worry. She pressed a

hand to the plastic. Alastair lifted his own and pressed it to meet hers.

The electric saw started, the loud noise echoing around them.

Then fresh air hit him and he breathed deep. Thom and Dec reached through the broken plastic and helped him out. He felt lightheaded but wasn't planning to admit that to anyone.

"Shit, man." Thom slapped his hand against Alastair's back.

"I'm fine, now," he assured them all.

Now that his head was clearing, all he could think about was the fact that the bastard could have taken Darcy instead of him. He guessed today's attacks were to issue warnings and scare the fuck out of both of them.

Darcy grabbed his hand, her fingers brushing his pulse. He saw a glimmer in her eyes.

"Don't you dare cry," he said.

"I'm not."

"I'm an only child. A woman's tears..." Left him feeling helpless and unmanned.

"He hands any crying witnesses over to me," Thom said, clearly trying to lighten the mood. "Completely useless."

Darcy sniffed.

"You're screwed now," Dec said. "She knows Cal and I can't handle tears, either. Woman can wield them like a weapon."

Her eyes narrowed. "I do not." Then she looked back at Alastair. "He needs to get checked out—"

"No. I'm fine."

"You made me get checked out."

"Chlorine gas exposure is a bit different to not having fresh air. I didn't even lose consciousness."

"You did from the stun gun."

"So did you."

"How about you both take the afternoon off and get some rest," Thom said.

Alastair scowled at his partner. "No, I—"

Thom held up a hand. "You—" he pointed at Alastair, then at Darcy "—and you. Go. Now. No arguments."

DARCY STEPPED out of the shower and wrapped herself in the dark-blue towel.

God, she'd just showered in Alastair Burke's glossy bathroom.

He lived in a one-bedroom condo in a converted warehouse just north of the city. He'd told her the place had once been a helicopter factory. She loved it. It reminded her of the old flour mill in Denver that she and her brothers had converted into the Treasure Hunter Security offices.

Alastair's place had loads of exposed brick, touches of black iron, and a bathroom done in masculine gray tiles.

She looked at her reflection in the foggy mirror. Her hair was wet, her face was makeup-free and pale. She had god-awful shadows under her eyes.

Dammit, Burke was right. It might only be the afternoon, but she needed some rest. She felt drained and still a little shaky from the chlorine attack. Not to mention the panic at seeing Alastair trapped in that box. She swallowed, feeling the raw sensation in her throat.

She pressed her hands to the sink and pulled in a breath. Memories crowded into her head. The horrible coughing, the choking, combined with knowing Silk Road had Alastair, and that damn ticking timer.

She looked back into the mirror. Nothing like black-market thieves repeatedly trying to kill you to put your life in perspective.

She was no longer the awkward, nerdy teen with the big, tough, overachieving brothers, or the completely-in-love, larger-than-life parents.

Darcy knew her own worth. She was damn good at her job, had skills that very few people possessed, and even without her makeup and her hair blow dried, she looked pretty good. And she wanted love and a family of her own.

She stepped into Alastair's bedroom. It was neat—no surprise there—and decorated in masculine colors with warm wood accents. Unrepentant about snooping, she opened a few drawers and looked in the closet.

One framed picture sat on the dresser. It showed a smiling woman in a simple dress and cheap shoes, hugging a serious-looking, dark-haired boy. The boy looked like he was about ten.

It was then she noted the intense green eyes.

God. The boy was a young Alastair. She peered closer. His face had the same impassive stare she looked at every day. A part of her had always wondered if he'd sprung into existence as a fully-formed adult with a gun on his hip.

This woman had to be his mother. Darcy ran a finger over the frame and wondered where the woman lived, and if she was close to her son.

Turning away, Darcy decided to find something to wear. Since she had no clean clothes, she had to borrow something. In the closet, she pulled a crisp, white business shirt off a hanger and slipped it on. It almost reached her knees.

She left her hair wet. There wasn't much she could do with it, anyway. And while she might sell her soul for her MAC collection, makeup-free was going to have to do until she got her things.

When she walked into the living area, a wonderful smell hit her. She halted. Burke was cooking. He'd taken his jacket off and had his shirt sleeves rolled up.

Darcy let out a shuddering breath. If men only knew how insanely attractive it was to a woman to watch a man cooking something up in the kitchen... And Alastair looked beyond fine, stirring a pot of something mouthwatering. *Whatever. He's still arrogant, bossy, and annoying, remember?*

He looked up and stared at her.

"Ah, I borrowed a shirt." She fought not to tug on the hem.

His eyes darkened. "So I see." He nodded at the stools on her side of the granite island. "Take a seat."

She pulled herself up, studying his face. He looked none the worse for wear for his ordeal.

"I hope you like fettuccine carbonara," he said. "I'm making a late lunch, or an early dinner."

She looked at him aghast. "You cook? Like, with ingredients?"

He turned to face her, and he looked outrageously scrumptious holding a wooden spoon.

"My mom taught me."

Darcy felt something change in the air between them. "I saw the picture in your room. That's her, right?"

He tensed.

"Sorry," she said. "I wasn't snooping." *Big fat liar, Darcy Ward.*

"Yeah. That's her."

"You're close?"

"We were."

His tone made goose bumps break out on Darcy's skin. Burke reached over, pulling open the stainless-steel refrigerator and pulling out a bottle of sparkling water. Next, he grabbed some tall glasses.

"Hope water's okay. I did some research, and you need to avoid alcohol for a little while."

Darcy took the glass. She should never have brought up the photo.

He leaned against the counter. "My mother was murdered when I was ten."

Oh. God. "I'm so sorry, Alastair." Without thinking, Darcy reached out, pressing her hand over his.

He nodded, then pulled away and turned back to the stove. "It was a long time ago."

He flicked off the burner, set out plates, and started serving up the food. He slid a plate of the creamy pasta in front of her, then leaned against the counter as he ate his.

Darcy tasted the pasta and swallowed a moan. "Oh, God, this is so good."

She got a flicker of a smile.

Then her belly cramped, and she set her fork down. She was hungry, but the stress of the day was still riding her. "Our plan to take down Silk Road is going to work."

"That a question or a statement?"

"A statement." She straightened. "Today was the last straw. We're going to get the Collector, and by this time next week, there will be no more Silk Road."

He nodded. "Yes."

Such confidence. Just that single word said with so much conviction. If she'd learned anything about Alastair Burke, it was that he was a man of his word.

"It's time," he said. "Silk Road has been destroying lives for decades. With the Collector assuming sole control, things will only get worse."

Darcy swallowed down another bite of pasta. "I agree, one hundred percent. They've been targeting my family and friends for a while. And now me and you."

She looked up and saw a muscle tick in his jaw.

She reached out and grabbed his hand again. "We'll stop them."

His thumb stroked her skin. "We will."

They finished eating, and Darcy insisted on helping him clean up. When she flopped onto the gray suede couch, she suppressed a grateful sigh. When she pulled out her tablet, it was whisked out of her hands.

"Hey—"

"No work. Rest."

She rolled her eyes and watched him tuck the device

away. She wasn't sure what to do with herself. There was no way she was admitting how tired she felt.

Alastair clicked on the television, and she leaned into the couch.

"I have some work to do," he said. "I'll be in my office, if you need me."

She watched him disappear through a set of double doors and fought a pout. Of course, *he* was allowed to work. She focused on the TV and a few minutes later she fell asleep.

Darcy blinked awake, a scream caught in her throat. She'd been having a nightmare about the attack. She'd been trapped in a plastic box filling with gas, Alastair trapped on the other side of the plastic.

She looked around and saw unfamiliar brick walls. She exhaled sharply and her brain finally caught up. *Alastair's place.*

She had no idea what time it was. It was dark outside the windows, the lights were on low, and the television was off. She pushed her hair off her face and spotted her suitcase sitting by the front door. She barely suppressed her cry of glee.

She got up and went looking for Alastair.

His office was dark and he wasn't at his desk.

She almost moved away, when she spotted a shadow sitting in an armchair in the corner of the room.

She stepped into the office. In the ambient glow from the living room, she saw he was sitting in the shadows, cradling a glass of whisky. His head was down.

"Alastair?"

He didn't move, but the brooding vibe hit her hard.

"You almost died today."

Darcy felt rooted to the spot, a knot in her chest. His deep, rasping tone made her throat tight. "You did too. And I'm fine. You came for me."

He looked up. "A few more minutes—"

She moved to him now. Right in this moment, there was no way she could resist the pull between them. She rested her hands on his shoulders. "I'm okay, Alastair. We're both okay."

He pulled in a deep breath and tipped his head back. Darcy didn't let herself think. She'd almost died and so had he. She reached down and cupped one stubbled cheek. She stepped between his legs, then she leaned down and kissed him.

He tasted so good, with an edge of whisky. He smelled as good as always—that crisp cologne that now always made her think of Alastair Burke. He didn't touch her, but he took over the kiss, his tongue sliding against hers.

She heard his glass hit the rug with a muffled thump. His hand came out and gripped her waist, tugging her roughly onto his lap. She made a hungry sound, sliding her hands into his hair.

"Darcy...damn..." One hand cupped her ass and kneaded. He kissed her again.

A phone started ringing.

No. She tightened her hands in his hair.

Alastair broke the kiss and cursed. "That's Thom's tone."

Struggling to find some control, Darcy pulled in a few breaths and slid off his lap. She stood on shaky legs.

"Thom?" A pause. "You ran the prints on the chlorine device and the box." Alastair's jaw tightened. "Nothing came up. Not a surprise." Another pause. "Okay, yeah, keep me informed."

Alastair slid the phone away, his gaze meeting hers.

"No evidence off the chlorine device or the plastic box," she said.

Alastair shook his head. "You need a good night's sleep."

"I'm not sure I can sleep...I keep remembering the attack." Her chest tightened. God, she did not need to have a panic attack.

A hand gripped hers, squeezed. Instantly, her chest loosened a fraction.

"You take the bed," he said. "I'll sleep on the couch."

"Alastair—"

"I'll be right here, Darcy." His green eyes glowed with his promise. "I'll make sure no one gets in here and no one disrupts your sleep."

The last of the tension in her eased. If there was one thing she was starting to learn, it was that she could trust this man.

CHAPTER SEVEN

Alastair took his time checking the security screens in the Dashwood security room.

"The cameras are working well, Agent Burke," one of the security team said. "All the areas of the main lobby are covered within an inch of their lives." The man smiled. "Ms. Ward has done a brilliant job. Way better than the system we had before."

Alastair nodded. That was why he'd hired her. "Thanks, Chris."

He strode out of the office and headed for the lobby. Stepping out into the center of the space, he visually checked the camera locations, the main display, and ran through where he'd have agents stationed on the night. The opening gala was only one day away.

"Hey." Thom fell into step with him. "Feeling all right?"

"If anyone asks me that question again..."

"Okay, okay. Darcy got the trackers from her contact. She's ready to put them on the diamonds and test them."

Alastair nodded.

Darcy. He'd checked on her several times during the night, watching as she'd slept in his bed. He couldn't fully describe how much he'd liked seeing her dark hair spread out on his pillow.

Fuck. Even now, his body responded. Seeing her in his shirt had been torture. The taste of her was still in his mouth. The woman sure could kiss.

"Alastair? Alastair?"

He blinked and saw Thom looking at him. "Yeah?"

"I was telling you that I got your tuxedo."

"Fine." He scowled. He didn't care about his tux—he cared about taking Silk Road down, keeping Darcy safe, and working out how to keep his hands off her.

Feminine laughter echoed through the space and made every cell in his body come to life. His gaze zeroed in on Darcy. She was joking around with some young geek from the Dashwood security team. She looked fully recovered from her exposure to the chlorine gas.

"Thanks, Thom," Thom muttered sarcastically. "I appreciate your help."

Alastair looked back at his partner. "Shopping doesn't get you commendations, Singh."

The younger man held up a hand. "My boyfriend loves my shopping skills, mainly because I do his shopping for him. I outdid myself with your tuxedo, even if I do say so myself. I'll send you the invoice." The man rubbed his hands together with glee.

"Your love of fashion is...disconcerting," Alastair said.

"And your workaholic tendencies are disconcerting." Thom turned his head, looking at Darcy. "Although, I'm all for you finding some other...personal hobbies." Thom smiled. "How was it having a roommate last night?"

With another scowl for his annoying partner, Alastair strode across the lobby toward Darcy.

"Hi," he said.

She straightened. "Hi, yourself."

"Thom said the trackers arrived."

She smiled, excitement radiating off her. She snatched up a small plastic case. "Animal came through."

She spun, her hip bumping Alastair's. Her touch felt like he'd been hit by lightning. He shoved his hands in his pockets to keep from touching her.

He wanted to touch her, more than anything, but he couldn't afford to be distracted right now. Not on the eve of implementing their plan. And as he'd already established, Darcy Ward was one big distraction.

She grabbed her tablet. "We putting these babies on the diamonds now?"

He nodded.

Dec appeared. "Darcy. Burke."

"Hi, big bro." Darcy gave her brother a quick hug. "You've been going through the plan for the THS team for tomorrow?"

He nodded. "Cal and I have it worked out." His gaze bored into Darcy. "I told him, and Mom and Dad what happened yesterday. They're worried."

"You told on me?" Darcy said.

"We all want you safe," Dec said. "I want you staying with me."

"I'm fine," she told him. "This is almost over, Dec."

"I want to keep an eye on you."

Burke moved closer, standing right behind Darcy. "I'm doing that."

That just made Dec's scowl deepen.

"When's the rest of the team getting here?" Darcy asked.

"I know you're changing the subject," Dec said. "This afternoon."

"Who's coming?"

"All of them."

Alastair raised his brows. "All of the Treasure Hunter Security team?"

"They all wanted in. They heard about the attacks on Darcy, and they've all had run-ins with Silk Road." Dec grimaced. "The wives and significant others are coming, too." He let out a sigh. "And Mom and Dad."

Darcy groaned. "We're supposed to be keeping a low profile at the gala."

"They can blend."

Darcy snorted. "Coop can, because he's a former spy. And Morgan can, because she's just badass. Hale and Cal, maybe. But Logan?"

Dec winced. "Sydney will be with him. She can tame him for a night."

"You're sure?" Burke asked.

"I'm sure." The man's face was serious. "We all want to be here for this."

And all the THS members were good. Burke wasn't going to turn down any help. He nodded. "We're heading down to the vault to place the trackers on the diamonds."

Dec looked back at his sister. "Please come and stay in my suite."

"And be the third wheel to you and Layne? I don't need to hear you doing the nasty with your wife. No, thanks." Darcy reached out and touched her brother's arm. "I'm safe."

"I hate the idea of you alone in a hotel room."

"Um..." She glanced at Alastair.

"She's staying with me," he said.

Dec went still. His gaze locked with Alastair's. "Think you and I need to have a chat."

"We can do that."

"What? No." Darcy stomped a foot. "I'm an adult woman, so you macho idiots are *not* having a chat." She swiveled. "I'm heading to the vault to work on the diamonds."

She stormed off, and Alastair caught up with her at the stairs. He decided it was best not to talk on the way down to the vault and simply let her walk off her pique.

He nodded to the guards as they entered the vault. At the table, he opened the diamond case.

Darcy smiled. "Looking at these never gets old."

The diamonds lay nestled safely in the case, gleaming under the lights.

"You like diamonds, Darcy?" He could picture her with a strand of them around her neck. And nothing else.

She smiled. "Every woman likes diamonds, Agent Burke. And if she tells you differently, she's lying." She studied the diamonds. "I've been doing more research on the gems, especially the Black Orlov."

"Trying to prove the curse?"

She turned to him. "I confirmed the death of the diamond dealer. A Mr. J.W. Paris. Shortly after he sold the Black Orlov, he jumped off a Manhattan skyscraper."

"My file says he had business problems."

Darcy leaned against the table. "Fifteen years after Mr. Paris died, the diamond belonged to a Russian princess, Princess Leonila Viktorovna-Bariatinsky. She also jumped to her death. Soon after, another Russian princess, Princess Nadia Vygin-Orlov, the wife of a Russian jeweler became the proud owner of the diamond."

"And its next 'victim.'"

Darcy nodded. "She jumped off a building in Rome."

"And since then, the diamond was re-cut in order to break the curse." He looked at the dark gem.

"What if it is some sort of ancient technology?" Darcy said. "Maybe a weapon."

He raised a brow.

"I tried to trace the earliest legends. It appears to have come from a shrine in Pondicherry, India. The uncut diamond was set in a statue—the Eye of Brahma, the Hindu creator god."

"Doesn't make it a weapon."

Her face lit up. "I discovered a few interesting things about Brahma. So first, he was the creator of all the gods, animals, men and women. But some legends say that he was worried about over population by immortals. He wanted balance, so he helped create Death, who in some legends was, of course, a woman."

"So the creator god was also known to cause death." Just like the diamond that bore his name.

"He was also the creator of the brahmastra," Darcy continued.

"Which was?" Alastair prompted.

"In Hinduism, astra were formidable weapons infused with supernatural power. THS ran across an astra in Antarctica recently, one that Silk Road was desperate to get their hands on. The vajra."

Alastair straightened and muttered a curse. His gaze fell on the black diamond. He'd read a report on Dec and Ronin Cooper's adventures in Antarctica.

Darcy nodded. "Team 52 confiscated it."

"And the brahmastra?" Alastair asked.

"There are lots of stories and legends. Some describe rods, spear tips, and glittering arrows. Others say it was a fiery weapon of destruction. Some stories just say it caused death to whoever was its target, or that it could destroy an entire army. Some legends describe powerful variants like the brahmashirsha astra and brahmanda astra. Weapons capable of destroying the world."

"Dammit."

She nodded. "Maybe this diamond is nothing but a unique gem." She winked. "Or maybe it really is cursed."

"Let's just make sure Silk Road doesn't ever get it," he said.

She set down the small case and opened it. Alastair frowned. He didn't see anything inside it.

"Where are—?"

Darcy held up a set of tweezers and reached into the case. When she lifted her hand, he saw a tiny, transparent circle on the end of the tweezers. It looked like a contact lens, but much smaller.

She turned and reverently put her other hand on the Regent, lifting it carefully from the case.

"Hold this for me." She handed the diamond to him.

Alastair clutched the blue diamond in his hand, holding it still as she attached the tracker. The diamond was cool against his skin. It was hard to believe it had once been touched by kings and queens.

She stepped back. "Done."

He peered closely. There was no sign of the tracker. "Incredible."

"I knew Animal could do it."

"I might need to recruit him."

She snorted. "Good luck with that."

Carefully, Alastair set the diamond back in the case.

"One down, two to go," she said.

Working together, they got the other two trackers attached.

Darcy stroked a finger over the Black Orlov. "So you really don't think it's cursed?"

"I don't believe in curses."

She grinned. "Of course, the sensible Agent Burke wouldn't believe in a curse. Do you think it has...abilities?"

"Probably not. But I'd prefer you quit touching it, so we don't test out that theory."

With a nod, Darcy pulled up her tablet. "Now for the moment of truth. Time to see if the trackers actually work."

DARCY TAPPED ON HER TABLET, trying to ignore Alastair's yummy cologne.

He was still holding the Orlov necklace draped over his palm. There was something strangely sinister about the gem, but it was definitely beautiful, as well.

She wondered if it had really driven several people to take their own lives and leap to their deaths.

"Okay, here we go," she said.

Her program came to life, the screen flickered, and a map showing the Dashwood layout appeared. Three glowing dots sat close together—the Regent, the Sancy, and the Black Orlov.

"Carry the necklace over there." She pointed across the room.

Alastair walked away. The dot on the screen moved.

She grinned. "It's working. Try heading out of the vault."

He stepped outside and she heard him talking with the guards. She followed the dot as it moved across the screen. Alastair reappeared.

"It looks good," she said.

All of a sudden, Alastair stiffened, then stared at the vault wall. He looked lost in thought.

"Burke?

No response.

Her pulse kicked, a chill shivering through her. "Alastair?"

He blinked.

"Alastair?" She gripped his arm.

He did another slow blink and looked at her. "You're happy with the tracker?"

"You just stopped and stared at the wall. You okay?"

His brow furrowed. "I did?"

She nodded.

"Just lost in thought, I guess." He set the Orlov back in the case and lifted the Sancy. He moved around the room, and the tracker worked like a charm. The same for the Regent.

She kept a sharp eye on Alastair, but he seemed fine. She shook her head. She was spooking herself with her own myths.

Alastair smiled at her. "You are brilliant."

Her belly flip-flopped. Oh, boy, that smile. She pretended to buff her nails on her shirt. "Of course, I am, Agent Burke." She turned her tablet off. "Now, I have a very important errand to run if I'm going to be prepared for tomorrow."

His brows drew together. "What? Is there more equipment you need?"

"Yes. I need a dress for the gala."

He stilled. "You want to go shopping?"

"I *always* want to go shopping."

"You'll take an escort."

Darcy cocked a hip. "Try that again."

"This is another of those situations where it's an order, Darcy." She opened her mouth, but he held up a hand. "No arguments."

"I was going to say 'sure.'"

He eyed her suspiciously. "Take Thom. He's the only agent I know who won't complain about watching you shop."

She smiled. "Thank you, Agent Burke."

His eyes flashed and he leaned closer. "Isn't it time you just call me Alastair?"

Her pulse tripped, and for a second, she thought he was going to kiss her. Or she was going to grab that shirt of his and wrinkle the hell out of him when she kissed him. "Alastair."

He stepped back. "I'll have Thom meet you at the front entrance."

Darcy watched him stalk away, and unrepentantly stared at his fine ass as he did. She blew out a breath. The man was under her skin, and the funny thing was, she wasn't all that upset about it, anymore.

About twenty minutes later, Darcy found herself pulling away from the Dashwood, with the ever-cheerful Agent Thomas Singh behind the wheel.

"Where to?" he asked

"The best shopping in DC, my friend. I need a dress."

His smile brightened. "Budget?"

She smiled. "I need a *rocking* dress. No budget."

Thom's smile got bigger. "I know just the place."

He took her to the Collection at Chevy Chase. The street was lined with high-end boutiques.

They moved in and out of the shops, spending several minutes in each one. Darcy knew just what she wanted, but she hadn't seen it, yet. She tried on a few things, but nothing was quite right. Thom was an excellent shopping partner and proved he had a good eye.

But she still hadn't seen *it* yet.

Then, she stepped into one more store, smiling at the well-dressed woman behind the counter. Her gaze fell on a dress displayed on a mannequin toward the back of the boutique.

Darcy sucked in a breath. That was it. "I'd like to try that one, please."

The saleswoman smiled. "It'll be perfect with your coloring."

Inside the dressing room, she zipped herself in, settling the neckline in place. Oh, man. She stepped out of the small cubicle.

Thom was on his phone, but when his head lifted and he spotted her, his jaw dropped open. "Holy shit." He ended his call.

"I think you just hung up on someone." Darcy spun, the mermaid bottom swishing around her legs. "You like?"

He blinked. "You'll bring him to his knees."

Darcy ran her hands down the sleek satin. "My dress selection has nothing to do with Special Agent Alastair Burke."

"Uh-huh. Sure." Thom winked. "You look like a million bucks, Darcy."

She looked at the price tag and winced, but then she looked at herself in the mirror again. She decided it was *so* worth it. So what if she had to eat toast for a few months when she got back to Denver.

Then she remembered that the gala wasn't just a party where she got to wear a fabulous dress. Damn, for a second, she'd forgotten about Silk Road.

"Darcy?"

She looked at Thom. "What if things go wrong

tomorrow?" She thought of Alastair or her brothers getting hurt. "What if—?"

"Hey." Thom touched her arm. "We're ready. We're prepared. We're going to get them. With you and THS onboard, we've got a hell of a team. And Alastair and I will make sure you don't get hurt."

Her heart clenched. She didn't want smiling Thom hurt, either. And she really, really didn't want the bossy, intelligent man who had burrowed impossibly deep under her skin getting hurt, either.

CHAPTER EIGHT

Alastair strode through the Dashwood's transformed lobby. Lights were on everywhere, setting the space gleaming. Guests milled around, wearing tuxedos, silk, satin, and lace. They chatted and sipped drinks from the loaded trays the servers carried through the crowd. A string quartet was playing in one corner.

Glancing toward the diamond display, flanked by large red banners, he saw that the main case was still covered with a black cloth for the unveiling. He spotted the museum's bigwigs, hobnobbing with several politicians and local celebrities.

But Alastair wasn't really concerned with who was here and what they were wearing. He scanned the space again, checking the security at the front entrance. Everyone was being wanded to ensure no weapons made it inside. He spotted Thom moving through the crowd, and nodded. He saw several other agents, as well.

He touched his earpiece. "Cameras?"

"All good," came the response from the security room.

Dec appeared out of the crowd. The rugged man cleaned up well, looking pretty at ease in his tuxedo. An attractive brunette in bronze silk was at his side—his archeologist wife, Dr. Layne Ward.

"Burke." Dec nodded.

"Evening." Alastair nodded at Layne. "Dr. Ward."

She smiled. "Layne. Please."

Dec's gaze moved over Alastair's tux. "You don't look like an FBI agent tonight."

"Thank my partner. He has an unhealthy obsession with clothing." Alastair's tux didn't look that different from any other in the room, except for the fact that it fit him perfectly and was clearly custom tailored. How the hell Thom had pulled that off without a fitting, he had no idea. Alastair turned, scanning the room again. "Have you seen Darcy?"

"She's on her way," Dec said.

A smile tipped Layne's lips. "Us girls spent some time getting ready together. It'll be worth the wait."

Alastair wasn't sure what to make of that smile, and looked back at Dec. "Your team is in place?"

The man nodded and discreetly pointed across the room.

Alastair spotted Darcy's other brother, Callum. He and Dec weren't quite identical, but it was clear that they were brothers. He was with his wife, Dani, a world-famous photographer. Apparently, the pair had recently been married by a monk in Tibet on one of their round-the-world trips. No surprise, she held a small camera and was taking photos, the lights glinting off her short, beaded, green dress. Her husband was watching her indulgently.

Then Alastair saw Logan O'Connor. He was a hard man to miss. Big, with his tawny hair brushing his shoulders, the man was scowling and tugging at his bowtie. Then Logan's gaze snagged on something and his face changed. Alastair blinked. The man's features filled with warmth and the guy was almost...smiling.

The crowd parted, and an elegant, slender blonde in a column of white silk and holding two glasses of champagne glided toward O'Connor. When she reached the man, he slid an arm around her waist and pulled her in for a kiss. God, they looked like beauty and the beast.

"Morgan and Zach are on the mezzanine," Declan said.

Alastair looked up. Morgan Kincaid was leaning against the railing. She was a tall, athletic brunette, and her short, aquamarine dress showed off her mile-long legs. A man leaned beside her, looking debonair in his tuxedo—archeologist Zachariah James. They were smiling at each other, as though they were sharing a private joke.

Alastair's gaze moved down the stairs from the mezzanine, and he spotted a small, fit woman with copper-colored hair. Her long black dress swished around her legs, and she tilted her head back to smile at the man by her side. Peri Butler—experienced polar guide. The dark-haired man with her was former SEAL and CIA agent, Ronin Cooper. Alastair was well aware that Cooper was not a man you messed with.

"Hello, Alastair."

The female voice behind him made him spin. As soon as his gaze fell on the blonde-haired woman in the pale-blue dress, delight hit him. There were days he still missed working with Special Agent Elin Alexander. He moved and pressed a quick kiss to her cheek.

Then he pulled back and looked at the handsome man standing beside her, with dark skin and a wide smile.

"I'm still unhappy with you, Hale," Alastair said. "You stole my best agent."

Hale Carter pulled Elin to his side. "She still works for the FBI, Burke." The big man smiled down at her, love on his face. "She just likes the Denver weather better."

Elin laughed, and Alastair's chest warmed. It was good to see her happy. For a long time, like Alastair, she'd lived only for her job and for revenge against Silk Road. Carter was a good man, and Alastair was pleased for her.

"Everything's in place?" Elin kept her voice low.

Alastair nodded. "We'll unveil the diamonds shortly, and then wait for the Collector to make his move." He looked at Dec again. "You said your parents were coming." He hadn't seen the Wards among the crowd.

"Right here, Agent Burke," an amused female voice said from behind him. "Were you afraid I was planning to steal something?"

He spun. Professor Oliver Ward, distinguished history professor, stood beside a small, compact woman dressed in midnight-blue. The professor had a handsome face and well-cut graying hair. The woman eyed Alastair boldly with gray eyes. Persephone Ward, renowned—or infamous—treasure hunter. Darcy's parents.

"Dr. and Mrs. Ward." He inclined his head. "Of course, I didn't think you'd steal anything." Perhaps the thought had crossed his mind.

Persephone Ward's smile said she knew exactly what he was thinking. "So you're the agent who's been driving my daughter crazy."

"Guilty." Alastair met the woman's stare. "To be fair, she does the same to me."

Oliver smiled and Persephone barked out a laugh.

Alastair looked around again. "Speaking of which, where is Darcy?"

Elin cleared her throat. "Here she comes."

Alastair turned and felt like the tiles under his feet tilted. His heart knocked hard against his ribs.

The crowd parted as she walked toward them. *Fucking hell.* He tried to breathe, but it was near impossible, his chest was locked too tight.

She wore silky, shiny red. The dress clung everywhere, but flared out at her feet. The neckline sat off her slim shoulders, showing way too much skin, and showcasing her gorgeous breasts.

"Breathe," Elin murmured, amusement in her voice.

He finally managed to drag in some air. Darcy's gaze locked with Alastair's and she shot him a sultry smile.

"Hi, guys."

"Darcy, you look amazing." Layne hugged her sister-in-law.

Alastair just stood there dumbly, watching as she greeted her family and friends. Pressure built inside him.

"You look gorgeous, my darling," Persephone drawled.

When blue-gray eyes met his again, he circled her arm. "We need to check on some security issues." He pulled her away from the group and around one of the columns.

Her brows drew together. "Hey—"

He spun her and backed her into the column.

She arched a brow. "I thought you wanted to check on security?"

She'd done something smoky to her eyes, and her lips were a brilliant red that matched her dress.

"You're trying to kill me, aren't you?" he growled.

Her face changed, looking very satisfied. "You think this little ol' dress is for you, Agent Burke?"

He pressed an arm against the marble above her head and leaned closer. She was wearing a different perfume tonight, something straight-up sexy, that filled his senses.

"Yes, I think it is."

Her teeth sank into her bottom lip. "Then you're right."

"You are so beautiful, Darcy." His breath mingled with hers, the air between them scorching hot. "I don't want anyone else to look at you."

"Caveman."

"That's how I feel, knowing every man in this room will be looking at you and imagining peeling that dress off your sexy body."

Her chest hitched. "Well, they can look, but they can't touch."

He lowered his voice, his blood pumping thickly through his veins. "Can I touch?"

Her eyelids flickered. "I'll think about it." She ran her nails up his shirt, fiddling with the buttons up to his bow tie. "You do look hot in a tuxedo. Thom picked it for you, didn't he?"

Alastair groaned. "We have a job to do. I need to stay focused." He made himself step back from the temptation of her.

Darcy took a few steps away with a whisper of silk. Then she paused and turned, shooting him a look over her bare shoulder. "Let's catch us some bad guys, Alastair, and then later, if you're lucky, maybe I'll do the touching."

DARCY DRAGGED in a deep breath and tried to focus. It was hard with wet panties.

She watched Alastair stalk off to check in with his agents. She hadn't been lying—the way the man looked in a tuxedo should be illegal. It fit his hard body like a glove. Her mouth watered and her ovaries sighed.

"You know, watching you look at him, and him look at you...I have to tell you, it makes me very hot and bothered."

Darcy spun, happiness bursting inside her. "Sloan!"

She hugged her friend. The woman's dark hair was styled in loose curls, and she was wearing a strapless dress in a deep purple.

"You look gorgeous, as always."

Sloan raised a brow. "You look hot enough to burn."

"What are you doing here?"

"I wanted to help back you up tonight. Without you, Silk Road would have killed Diego and me. So, we're here to help."

Darcy would have preferred her friend be far away and safe back in Miami. But Sloan was an experienced DEA agent and could more than handle herself.

Darcy looked around. "So, where is your hot guy?"

A smile curled Sloan's lips. "He went to say hello to Declan."

Darcy followed her friend's gaze and once again, her ovaries quivered. Diego Torres was one fine male specimen. He had brown skin, tousled brown hair, and a sexy smile. The SEAL-turned-salvage captain wasn't wearing a tux, but looked mighty fine in a blue suit, with a crisp white shirt and no tie. Mr. Cool.

"Sloan, if you weren't my best friend, I'd steal your man," Darcy said.

Sloan sipped her champagne. "Oh?" The brunette smirked. "Then I might just need to sample a certain hot, rugged FBI agent."

Darcy made a noise. "Try and I'll take you down."

Sloan laughed.

Darcy scanned the room and instantly she found him. He was on the stairs, giving orders as usual, to a couple of his agents. So damn handsome. She'd bet he was bossy in bed too. Her belly quivered. And she was really desperate to find out.

"I need a cigarette again," Sloan said.

Darcy slapped her friend's arm just as Diego reached them.

"Hi, Diego."

"*Hola*, Darcy." He smiled at her and pressed a kiss to her cheek. "You look incredible." He lifted his gaze and did a quick scan of the party.

Darcy grinned. You could take the SEAL out of the Navy, but you couldn't take the SEAL out of the man.

"Everything good?" he asked.

"So far." At that moment, a rush of nerves hit her. She'd been so focused on Alastair, and him seeing her dress, that she'd used it as an excuse not to let nerves set in.

She pulled in a breath. She'd channel it. Taking down Silk Road was the number-one priority, and they were making that happen. Tonight.

"Ladies and gentlemen." The Director of the Dashwood Museum, Mr. Linus Monroe, was standing at the podium, his voice echoing across the lobby. "Welcome to the opening of a truly fascinating exhibit. A generous donor has opened his private collection, and is sharing these fascinating treasures with us."

As the guests clapped, Darcy sensed Alastair move up behind her.

"And thanks also to cooperation with a fellow, world-class museum in France...you probably wouldn't know its name."

Polite laughter.

The director smiled and waved a hand. "Our special thanks go to the Louvre, for their generosity in loaning us some very unique, exquisite gemstones to complete the exhibit. Therefore, ladies and gentlemen, it is my great pleasure this evening to unveil the Cursed Diamonds Exhibit."

A spotlight shone on the diamond case, still draped in the black cloth.

Without thinking, Darcy reached out and grabbed Alastair's hand.

This was it. A sense of excitement moved across the crowd, and she heard a few titters. Alastair's fingers clenched on hers.

The director gripped the black cloth and then whipped it off.

Almost as one, the crowd gasped.

In the clear display, the diamonds glinted.

"Ladies and gentlemen, I give you three priceless treasures: the Sancy, the Regent, and the Black Orlov."

Applause and cheers erupted.

The lights went off, plunging the museum into pitch blackness.

CHAPTER NINE

Every muscle in Alastair's body went on high alert.

A light flared to life beside him, and he saw that Darcy had pulled her tablet from somewhere and turned it on.

"Accessing the system now," she murmured.

The museum's emergency lighting came on—small lights at the base of the walls—casting a dim glow in the lobby.

"Dim the tablet," he said. He didn't want her to stand out as a target.

The light dimmed to almost nothing.

He shifted closer to her, feeling her warmth pressed against him. "The diamonds?"

"Still in their case."

All around them were confused murmurs.

Alastair pressed a finger to his earpiece. "Thom? Thom?" Nothing. "Comms are being jammed."

Darcy muttered a creative curse. "Bastards shouldn't be able to do that. Let me see what I can do about it."

"What the hell is going on?" someone shouted.

"Everyone stay calm," Burke called out.

"Power to the main lighting system is down," Darcy whispered. "They aren't in the system, so my guess is that they've disrupted power *outside* the museum. But this definitely wasn't an accident."

Alastair had never thought it was.

"Cameras are still operational. Switching to the night vision cameras now."

He saw the screen of her tablet change to a dark image with a familiar, eerie green tinge.

She grabbed his sleeve. "Alastair, I can see figures moving through the crowd—"

He saw them, too—moving with purpose and no hesitation.

Bang.

Stun grenades started going off—sharp bangs and piercing flashes of light. *Bang. Bang.* Screams echoed through the lobby.

Alastair dived on top of Darcy, taking her down to the ground. He covered her, but could still see her tapping frantically on her tablet.

"Yes! I got comms back."

Brilliant woman. "Thom?"

"Here. We're moving to neutralize." Thom sounded focused but pissed. "You okay?"

"Yeah. Ward? You there?"

"My team is moving in, too." Ward sounded like he was ready to kick some ass. "You got eyes on Darcy?"

"She's with me and fine."

Gunfire. The rumble of the crowd turned terrified, punctuated with screams and shouts. *Fuck.* Alastair gritted his teeth. There shouldn't be weapons in here. They'd wanded everyone.

"How did they get guns and grenades in?" Darcy said.

"I'll find out," he said grimly.

Panic was setting in. The screams escalated and people were pushing.

He needed Darcy somewhere safe, not here where she could be trampled or hit. He levered off her and yanked her to her feet. "We need to move."

He pulled her along, pushing through the frantic crowd. He moved them toward the back of the lobby. In the darkness, he spotted the museum information desk and the area leading to the restrooms.

More gunfire, this time nearby. He yanked her around one of the columns, pressing her into the pillar. "Wait here."

He pulled out his Glock. In the glow of her screen, he saw Darcy nod. Her eyes were wide, but she was as steady as steel. He touched her chin, and she went up on her toes and pressed a kiss to his lips.

"Do your thing, Alastair. And be careful."

God, she was something. He pulled in a deep breath, let it out, and slid around the pillar.

He saw the man firing nearby. At least the bastard was shooting up at the ceiling and not into the crowd. He was only trying to cause panic, not kill. At the moment.

Alastair crept closer. Silently, he moved in behind the

man. He landed a hard chop to the back of the man's neck. The gunman stumbled forward with a groan, his weapon clattering on the tiles.

Alastair followed through with a hard punch and the man crumpled to the floor, out cold. Quickly, Alastair yanked zip ties out of his pocket and secured the man. The guy was dressed in a tux, so Alastair guessed Silk Road had snuck in posing as guests.

He grabbed the man's handgun. It was a strange design and light. That's when Alastair realized what it was—a 3D printed weapon made entirely of plastic. *Shit.*

There was still screaming, shouting, and gunfire. But now he heard the distinct sounds of hand-to-hand fighting as well. His team and THS had engaged.

He touched his ear. "Thom?"

"Here."

"They have 3D printed weapons."

His partner's curse echoed along the line. Somewhere nearby, another stun grenade went off and more screams erupted.

"Warn the team," Alastair said.

"On it. Alastair, the entrances have also been blocked from the outside."

Fuck. "Acknowledged. Let's get those bastards contained. I don't want anyone injured."

He hurried back to the column where he'd left Darcy. His chest contracted.

She wasn't there.

There was a faint line of light on the floor. He went down on one knee and his gut cramped.

It was her tablet, lying facedown on the floor, emitting a glow.

No.

He snatched up the tablet, then lifted his head and scanned the area.

He heard a feminine grunt and a scuffle from nearby. His jaw tightening, he lifted his weapon and followed.

DARCY STRUGGLED with the man dragging her away.

Asshole.

He'd surprised her and had hit her in the belly. *Hard.*

"Move faster," the man growled.

"I can't walk any faster in these heels, buddy." It was a lie, but he wouldn't know.

He yanked her roughly, almost sending her flying. She was close enough that she saw he was wearing a black silk scarf over the bottom half of his face. Oh yeah, Silk fucking Road. He was also in a tuxedo, so she figured they'd snuck in dressed as guests.

She kept dragging her feet. She just needed an opening, and then she was taking him down. "Just let me go. I've got nothing you want."

"We know who you are, Ms. Ward."

As he pulled on her arm again, her hip banged into what she guessed was the information desk. "So you know that my brothers, and THS, and the FBI are going to come looking for me?"

"We need to make use of your fancy computer skills."

"I'll *never* help Silk Road." Hell, she'd just make her own opening.

She pretended to stumble, and rammed into his stocky body. Her fingers brushed the butt of a holstered gun.

Yes. She reached for it.

But before she could yank it from the holster he spun, striking out at her. She whipped her arm up and blocked the blow. Pain vibrated up her arm, making her wince. The asshole was strong.

Well, lucky that Dec had taught her that winning a fight had nothing to do with physical strength.

She jabbed the heel of her flat palm against his throat.

He made a choking sound, but it was dark, and her aim was off. She knew it hadn't hit hard enough to debilitate. She jammed her foot down, ramming her heel into his ankle.

He staggered back. "Bitch."

"Yeah, when I need to be. Like when I have to deal with thieving bastards like you."

He came at her with a growl. Darcy spun and landed a punch to his kidneys. He grunted and as she turned again, he sank a hand into her hair.

Ow. He pulled her closer, rough fingers at her neck. She twisted and kicked, trying to break his hold. He pushed down on her skin.

A painful, electric feeling winged through her body. *Ow again.*

Then her legs went lax. *No.* He'd hit some nerve or pressure point. She sagged against him and her vision greyed. She desperately tried to fight off unconsciousness.

Suddenly, a dark shadow moved out of the gloom and slammed into the man.

The Silk Road thug released her and she slid to the floor. Looking up, Darcy could just make out Alastair and the man trading hard punches in the emergency lighting.

The sound of fists hitting flesh and pained grunts made her wince. She needed to help Alastair. She pushed up on her knees.

Hands grabbed Darcy's arm, pulling her up.

"No!" She swiveled. A dark shape loomed over her, another black scarf covering this guy's face. She yanked her dress up and kicked out at him, landing a very sharp heel in his thigh.

The man staggered back and pulled out a handgun. He aimed it at her and her blood turned to ice.

Shit. What now?

Alastair slammed into the man like a footballer on the field. They crashed into a column and she gasped.

Then, a sharp blow hit the back of Darcy's head and pain exploded through her. She fell forward, landing on her hands and knees.

"No," Alastair cried.

Through her blurring vision, she watched him spin and run to her.

God, he was handsome. He dropped down beside her, pulling her into his arms.

"Darcy."

That's when she saw both Silk Road thugs advancing. Just before she passed out, she saw an odd-looking gun pressed to the back of Alastair's head.

No. Then there was only darkness.

CHAPTER TEN

Alastair stroked Darcy's silky hair. "Wake up, baby. Please."

They'd been locked in a fucking janitor's closet. It was a small space that smelled like bleach and other chemicals. He couldn't see a thing, since the only light was the faint line coming from under the locked door.

He held Darcy's lax body in his lap. She hadn't regained consciousness and his gut was a mass of knots. He couldn't see her, but he could feel her chest rising and falling. He kept stroking her hair.

She'll be fine. She has to be. He felt the lump at the back of her head. It was swollen, but not bleeding.

The Silk Road men had taken his phone, earpiece, and weapon. They'd also taken Darcy's tablet.

Now he was trapped here, helpless. Ugly memories stirred. From another time, when he'd been locked in a closet. Another time that a woman he cared about had been hurt. His lungs constricted, his breathing harsh.

He tried to slow his breaths. *In, out. In, out.* He stroked Darcy's smooth cheek, and that small touch helped his chest loosen. He cared about smart, sassy Darcy Ward. A lot.

Alastair hadn't let himself care about anyone, not in a deep way, for a long time. Hell, ever.

Right now, all he wanted was for her to wake up. The ugliness he always kept at bay—the anger, the fear, the pain—welled inside him. He tried to push it down, but it loved the darkness. It always tried to push through in the middle of the night, in a tense situation, when he was alone.

Outside the door, he heard sporadic gunfire, and screaming. Cursing, he tightened his hold on Darcy. "Please wake up, baby." *Don't leave me here in the dark.*

He felt her stir in his arms.

His pulse leaped. "Darcy?"

She made a small sound, her hands gripping his forearm. "Oh my God, I can't see."

"We're locked in a closet. No lights."

"Fucking Silk Road," she muttered. "Are you okay?"

He touched her cheek. "You're the one that got a blow to the head, so that's my line."

"Last thing I remember is you with a strange gun to your head."

"I'm fine." He had a bruise forming where one guy had hit him, and a few other aches under his shirt, but nothing too bad. His tuxedo was ripped, and he was sure that Thom would be pissed. Alastair swallowed, his gut and chest still tight. "They're using plastic 3D printed weapons."

"Ah, explains how they got them through security. I thought even the best plastic weapons still had a few metal components?"

"Guess Silk Road perfected the design."

"Seems I'm in your lap again," she murmured.

She moved to sit up and he helped her. When she tried to move away, he tightened his arm, keeping her nestled in his lap. He needed to keep a hold on her to know she was okay, to keep those fucking old memories from slamming into him.

"I like you here."

He felt her go still. God, he wished he could see her face. His breathing turned harsh again. He'd come close to losing her. Again.

"Alastair? Are you sure you're okay?"

He couldn't get the words past the lump in his throat. Instead, he held her tighter and buried his face in her hair.

"You're so tense." She turned, her hands sliding across his shoulders. "Breathe, honey. We're okay."

"This is a pretty bad situation." His voice harsh. "I never wanted people put at risk like this."

She touched his cheek, like her fingers were memorizing his face in the dark. "But that's not it, is it?"

He wondered how she could read him so neatly when she couldn't even see him. He let out a shuddering breath. "You know my mother died."

"Yes."

"Silk Road killed her."

"What?" Darcy whispered.

"They attacked us in our apartment. They locked me

in a closet. I saw through a crack as three men questioned her. Tortured her. Then they shot her in the head."

"Oh, Alastair." Darcy wrapped her arms around him.

"She'd picked up a vase at a flea market. Paid three bucks for it. She was always doing stuff like that. Combing through other people's junk and things they'd tossed away, trying to find a pretty bargain. We were poor, but she tried to make our apartment pretty." Another shuddering breath. "She thought the vase was pretty. Turned out it was actually a Ming Dynasty vase, worth millions."

"I'm so sorry, honey." Darcy pulled his face to her chest.

He breathed her in, and for the first time since he'd lost his mother, he leaned in and took comfort from someone else.

They stayed there for a moment, then more gunfire sounded. This time much closer.

Alastair fought off the old emotions. He had to get Darcy to safety. His mind cleared. "We need to get out of here."

"I assume you tried the door?" Darcy asked.

"Locked. With the power down, the electronic locking system is offline." All the museum doors needed keycards or fingerprints to open them. "And they took my phone and your tablet."

She made a small sound. "Lucky I always carry a backup, then."

Alastair froze. "In that dress?"

"I'm hiding a few things under here."

The sultry tone made his cock rock hard and he swallowed a groan. He couldn't believe he was getting turned on in a situation like this. Still, this was Darcy they were talking about.

She shifted in his lap, and he heard the slide of silky fabric. He realized she was pushing the hem of her dress up.

"Darcy—"

"Stay focused, Alastair."

"You're killing me."

"We have bad guys out there and people who need our help."

He moved his hand and encountered smooth skin. He gripped her knee. She was reaching for something near her inner thigh. His cock throbbed and he bit back a groan. Unable to stop himself, he stroked the back of her knee.

Air puffed from her lips. "Hey, focus, remember? Gosh, no wonder you haven't caught Silk Road, yet. You're easily distracted."

"Only by you."

She stilled. "Don't be sweet when we're in a bad situation and I can't see you." She held something up and a light flicked on. He saw she was holding some sort of slim device. He realized it was a mini-tablet the size of a credit card. He watched her expand the device and tap on the screen.

"Okay, I'm sending a message to Dec," she said. "Where are we, exactly?"

"Janitor's closet near the information desk."

She tapped again. "Done."

"Where the hell were you hiding that? How were you hiding it under that dress?"

In the faint light, he saw her saucy wink. "One of my many secrets, Agent Burke."

Alastair suddenly wanted to know all her secrets. He wanted to know everything about this woman—her dreams, her wants, what made her laugh, what made her sigh.

"Now, how about we get out of here?" She stood, her dress swishing back down to her ankles. She moved over to the electronic door lock panel, plugged her tablet in, and set to work.

"You can get the locks back online?" He rose.

She didn't look up. "Probably not all of them from here, but I should be able to hack this one."

When he'd first seen Darcy tonight, he'd been knocked senseless by her beauty.

But seeing her like this, eyes alight with concentration and that fierce intelligence, it turned him on just as much.

"Got it!" She looked up and smiled.

There was a click and the door opened.

Alastair grabbed her and pressed a hard kiss to her lips. When he pulled back, he was pleased to see she looked dazed. "Stay behind me."

"Sure thing," she said.

He paused. "You're not lying, are you?"

Her pretty features smoothed out. "Who me? Of course not."

He shook his head. "Liar."

"You're such a smooth-talker, Agent Burke."

They cautiously moved back into the lobby and chaos. It was still dark, and smoke from the grenades hung in the air. There were pockets of fighting, and he knew his agents and THS were working to contain the situation.

He felt Darcy's fingers slip into the belt loops on his pants. They moved forward. He needed to find Thom and his agents.

Suddenly, Darcy jerked on his waist. "Alastair." Her tone was urgent.

"What?"

She reached around him and tilted her mini-tablet so he could see.

What he saw made his body lock. The three glowing dots were moving.

"The diamonds," she hissed.

Fuck. "Come on."

DARCY FOLLOWED Alastair as he pushed through the crowd. All around, guests were crouched and hiding. Some were silent and others were sobbing.

Well, this gala was going to be front page news.

More gunfire came from somewhere and she ducked. Alastair gripped her arm. God, Darcy hoped all the guests were okay. They'd known Silk Road would make a play for the diamonds, but not like this.

She looked back at her mini-tablet and saw the diamonds moving upstairs. "Diamonds are heading up to the mezzanine."

Alastair swiveled. In the faint emergency lighting, she saw the shadow of a big man jogging up the stairs.

Then Alastair sprinted forward. He took the stairs two at a time.

Dammit. Darcy hurried to follow after him. She just made out Cal and Logan in the shadows, fighting with some Silk Road men.

She knew the rest of the THS team would be spread throughout the room, fighting to bring Silk Road under control. She sent a silent prayer that they were all okay.

She was halfway up the stairs, when she saw Alastair reach the top. He tackled the man with the diamonds and she lost sight of them.

Lifting her skirt, she moved faster, and made it to the mezzanine. Ahead, Alastair and the man were circling each other. They charged, fists flying.

The blows were hard and powerful. A glancing hit caught Alastair on the chin and she winced. He dodged another punch, then rammed one into the Silk Road man's gut. The man doubled over, and Alastair kicked him.

Then she saw the glint of something in the man's hand. Her pulse went haywire.

"Alastair! He has a knife."

The man slashed out. Alastair leaped back, but he wasn't quite fast enough. There was enough light for her to see the huge tear across Alastair's shirt.

God, no. Darcy grabbed a nearby chair and charged.

"What the fuck?" The man turned, just as she rammed the chair into him.

"Darcy, back," Alastair bit out.

Momentum carried her forward. She ran the Silk Road man into the mezzanine railing.

He grunted, then gripped the chair and tore it away from her. He tossed it and it hit Alastair, who staggered back.

Darcy kept her gaze on the man. He was little more than a shadow. She saw the flash of the small metal case bulging in the inside pocket of his jacket. *The diamonds.*

She darted forward and grabbed the case.

A hard hand clamped onto her wrist and she grimaced. She could almost feel the delicate bones grinding together.

The man shoved hard and they lurched. She tried to pull the case closer, but he pulled back, pain flaring in her wrist.

"You're not stealing these," she snapped.

"I already have." He had a deep Southern twang.

He shoved harder, and they twirled like dancers. Her hip hit the railing. Hard.

"Where's the Collector?" she said.

"Waiting for me to deliver these."

She refused to let go of the case and they spun in another unwieldy circle. Annoyed, Darcy shoved the man and he leaped up onto a chair, towering over her.

"Darcy." Alastair rushed forward, grabbed a fistful of her dress, and yanked her back. Her fingers slipped off the case.

When she lifted her head, she watched the Silk Road man lift a gun. He pointed it straight at Alastair.

Her chest locked.

The man fired.

"No!" Darcy screamed. She watched as Alastair staggered back and fell to the floor.

Anger exploded through her and her vision turned red. Silk Road had already taken too many lives. They'd already taken Alastair's mother, they weren't taking him as well.

Without thinking, she shoved the Silk Road man in the gut with all her weight behind her.

He tipped backward and hit the railing.

Then he stared straight at Darcy, his face going lax. "Need to jump. We need to jump."

Her pulse leaped. "What?" His voice had lost its accent and sounded monotone.

He let himself fall back over the railing.

Oh, crap. Darcy leaned out, reaching for the case of diamonds.

The man grabbed a handful of her dress. *Shit.* He yanked her over the railing with him.

Shock blasted through her.

"Darcy!" Alastair's shout.

But then she was falling from the mezzanine. The Silk Road man let go of her and pointed his arms above his head like he was diving.

She threw her hands out. When her fingers brushed fabric, she clenched her hands closed.

It was one of the banners announcing the exhibit. She yanked on it, gripping hard. Her weight made it swing out from the side of the mezzanine.

Hell. She flew through the air and held on, sliding down the silky fabric.

The next second, her heels hit the tile floor and she

bent her knees. She didn't even fall over. She stood there, her heart hammering like an out-of-control drum.

Oh, God. She'd made it. She hadn't smashed into a thousand pieces on the tiles.

She looked over, and her gaze fell on the Silk Road man. Her belly turned over, nausea rising in her throat. He hadn't been so lucky.

In the emergency lighting, she could see him, lying flat on his back, his limbs bent at odd angles. She sucked in some breaths, trying not to be sick.

Then, a shadow swooped in. The newcomer leaned over the dead man and grabbed the case of diamonds from the man's pocket. His blond hair glinted as he turned and ran.

Shit. "Hey!"

CHAPTER ELEVEN

Ignoring his burning shoulder, Alastair leaped down the stairs.

Darcy had fallen off the fucking mezzanine. His heart was lodged in his throat. Fear pounded through him, leaving his mouth dry.

"Burke."

Declan was standing in the shadows at the base of the stairs. Alastair shouldered past him. He had to get to Darcy.

Suddenly, the lights clicked on.

All around, guests rose, blinking and clutching each other.

But his gaze was drawn to Darcy.

The air rushed out of him, leaving him lightheaded. She stood there in her beautiful dress. A little rumpled, but perfectly fine.

She wasn't lying on the ground, broken, like he'd

imagined in his head. Like the Silk Road fucker just behind her.

Her gaze moved to his torn shirt and shoulder. "Are you okay? That asshole shot you!"

"Just a graze."

She released a breath and smiled. "You should have *seen* my landing." She pointed to the banner that was lying on the ground, and he realized she must have used it to break her fall.

"Alastair." Thom appeared out of the crowd, gun drawn.

Alastair ignored him and strode toward Darcy. Fuck. *Fuck.* As he got closer, her eyes widened.

He pulled her into his arms, swept her back, and slammed his mouth down on hers.

She was frozen for a beat, then her hands clutched his shoulders and she kissed him back.

More than desire pounded through him. His need was stronger than just sex or attraction. He didn't know how long he kissed her, absorbing the warmth and life of her, but then he heard the sound of someone clearing their throat.

Reluctantly, he raised his head. He looked at her flushed face and swollen lips before lifting his gaze. He saw not just one, but two angry brothers pinning him with furious stares.

Great. But Alastair didn't give a fuck. Darcy was alive. That was all he cared about.

The Wards were standing behind their sons. Oliver's face was impassive, but Persephone was grinning.

"Well, this party has been *way* more interesting than I anticipated," the treasure hunter said.

Agents and security guards swarmed around. Nearby, Thom was yelling out orders as they rounded up the last of the Silk Road attackers. Others were helping the guests and shepherding in the paramedics and police.

Alastair tucked Darcy close to his side. "Thom, sitrep?"

"Thankfully, no casualties," his partner said. "A few injuries."

"Diamonds?"

"Someone grabbed them off him." Darcy nodded at the dead man on the floor without looking at him. "It was the weirdest thing, but he...wanted to jump."

Alastair couldn't care less about the man who'd pulled her over the edge. "Did you see the person who took the diamonds?"

"I didn't get a clear look, but he had blond hair. He ran." She held up her mini-tablet. "The trackers are active."

"Let's take this to the security room," Alastair suggested.

Dec stepped in front of him. "We're going to have a discussion." The man's eyes slid to his sister then back to Alastair. Beside Dec, Cal crossed his arms over his chest.

"Hello?" Darcy said. "Stolen priceless diamonds and black-market bad guys to sort out." She shot her brothers a glare, then turned to Alastair. "I'm sorry about the diamonds, Alastair."

"Don't be. This was the plan."

She stiffened, her head tilting slowly. "Excuse me?"

"I want the Collector. To do that, I need him out in the open."

Dec nodded. "And the only way to do that was to let them take the diamonds."

Darcy pressed her hands to her hips. "You *wanted* Silk Road to steal the diamonds?"

Alastair nodded. "And take them to the Collector."

She moved, pressing her hands to his chest and shoving him. "Why didn't you tell me?" she yelled.

"I couldn't risk any leaks—"

She hissed. "I've been working on this project for days! You really thought I'd blab about this?"

He grabbed her wrists gently. "No. I didn't tell anyone."

"Including me," a scowling Thom added.

Darcy wagged a finger at Alastair. "You and I are going to discuss this habit of keeping secrets."

"All right, let's get to the security room," Thom said.

"In a second." Alastair pulled Darcy closer. "First, I want Darcy to get checked out by the paramedics."

Her gaze fell to his shoulder. "I'm not the one who's bleeding."

"Flesh wound. You fell over a balcony." He managed to keep his voice relatively calm. "You'll get checked out."

Her eyes flashed. "Try that again, Agent Burke."

He leaned closer. "Darcy, will you please get checked out by the paramedics, since those Silk Road bastards hit a pressure point on your neck and you lost consciousness. Then one of them pulled you off the mezzanine, and took a fucking decade off my life."

All around, people were watching their conversation. Dec and Cal's expressions had darkened even more.

"Darcy, honey." Her father's tone was completely unruffled, like this happened all the time. "Please get checked out."

"Get checked, darling," Persephone added. "Your hot guy did ask very nicely."

"He did pretty well." Darcy tossed her head, her glossy hair swinging. "Fine."

Alastair smiled at her. Finally, he'd gotten his way.

THEY WERE all crammed into the Dashwood security room, staring at the big screens on the wall.

The paramedics had given Darcy a clean bill of health, and she'd then demanded they clean the flesh wound on Alastair's shoulder and check where he'd been attacked with the knife. Thankfully, while the knife had slashed his shirt, it hadn't reached his skin.

The panicked museum director was standing nearby, looking ill. Thom had re-acquired Alastair's phone and Glock, and Darcy's tablet from the now-arrested Silk Road thugs.

"The diamonds have stopped moving," Thom said.

Darcy leaned forward. Alastair was right behind her —big and protective.

"The Adana Tower," Alastair said.

Thom whistled. "Fancy. Exclusive residences for the rich and the ultrarich."

"What floor?" Alastair asked.

"Penthouse."

"Owner?"

Darcy tapped on her tablet, running a search. "Corporation called Elettaria, Inc."

"I haven't seen that one among Silk Road's long list of dummy companies. Track it down, and confirm it's them. I want a name." Alastair speared Thom with a look. "Get a judge out of bed. We need a search warrant."

His partner nodded. "It'll take time. It's midnight. By the time we get them up and put everything together—"

"Just do it."

"I doubt we'll have anything before morning, you know grumpy judges don't lose too much sleep over stolen relics."

"Silk Road is made up of murderers and thieves."

"I'm on it," Thom said.

Darcy frowned, staring at the image of the Adana Tower. She wanted to get in there now. The Collector was in there and they all knew it.

"I want all entrances and exits to the tower monitored," Alastair ordered. "And get a team into a neighboring building. I want full surveillance set up."

Thom nodded again.

"My team will work with your people on site," Dec said.

Alastair nodded, scowling at the screen. "Darcy, make sure the teams have access to the diamond trackers."

She nodded. "Done. What now?"

"Now you get some sleep," he answered.

She made a scoffing sound. "There is no way I could sleep."

"You want to help bring them down, you need some rest." He looked around. "Everybody does. I want a fresh team on the night watch, and everyone else rested so once we get the warrant, we're ready to go in."

As people shuffled out, Darcy crossed her arms over her chest. "You're resting too, right?"

"I need to check with the onsite team—"

She lifted her chin. "Then I'm coming, too. I'll rest when you rest."

His eyes flared and he looked at the ceiling. Then he met her gaze. "Please."

"This is one of those times where this is an order, Alastair."

She could tell he was gritting his teeth. His gaze ran over her, and then his face softened a little. "Deal."

Huh, she'd won for once. But watching him, heat flared to life inside her. She got the feeling he wasn't thinking about actually resting.

Darcy said good night to her family, hugging her parents and sisters-in-law. Her bossy brothers got scowls.

Alastair was quiet on the drive back to his place, except to take several calls updating him on the teams setting up at the Adana Tower. Once they were inside his condo, she sauntered across the living room, more than ready to kick off her heels.

He flicked a lamp on. "Darcy."

One word, but that tone shivered through her, setting every nerve alight. She turned.

His intense green gaze was on her, sliding down her

body. She shivered. His eyes were filled with heat and hunger.

"You put yourself in danger tonight." His voice was low.

Goose bumps broke out on her skin. "And someone shot you and tried to cut you up with a knife."

"Someone dragged you off the fucking second story." Alastair stalked toward her, shrugging out of his tuxedo jacket. He tossed it aside.

Darcy backed up, excitement skittering through her veins. She hated to admit it, but she was a little nervous, as well. This man was so intense.

The back of her knees hit the couch and she sat down automatically.

Alastair stopped in front of her, leaning over her.

"You don't risk yourself. *Ever*."

Her chest was rising and falling fast. She shifted. She was so turned on. That bossy, arrogant tone drove her insane.

"I'm not good at following orders, remember," she murmured.

"I do."

She ran her gaze over him, taking in that hard, rugged face, the torn and blood-stained shirt. God, he was gorgeous. Her eyes reached waist level and she saw the bulge there. Hunger made her ache.

She looked up and saw he was watching her. "Are you going to make me follow your orders?"

He made a harsh sound, and her gaze dropped again. The bulge behind his zipper was growing. He was hard for her.

His green eyes blazed hot. "Darcy." His voice was deep and thick, filled with dark promise.

She reached for him. She took a second to unbuckle his belt, flick open the button, and lower his zipper. She saw the muscles in his thighs flex under his trousers.

Her pulse was hammering as she pulled his cock free. *Oh, God.* His cock was beautiful. Thick, long, and hard. She wrapped her fingers around him.

"You like that?" His voice was gritty.

"Yes." She ran her hands up his hard length.

"You want my cock, Darcy?"

"Yes."

"Then show me."

With a moan, she leaned forward and licked the swollen head. The musky taste of him filled her and she moaned again.

He groaned, his hips moving forward.

Darcy opened her mouth and sucked him in. He muttered a curse, his hips bucking. Then he slid a hand in her hair and fed more of his cock into her mouth.

"Fuck. I've imagined this so many damn times."

She looked up, saw his gaze locked on where her mouth was wrapped around him. She moaned again, desire blazing through her. She sucked, loving knowing that she was driving this controlled man crazy.

"Imagined laying you out on your desk," he continued. "Getting my mouth between your legs."

She squirmed on the couch, aching between her legs. She hurt for him. She started to push her dress up, needing to ease the pain.

"No." He pulled out of her mouth. "You don't get to

come yet. You don't get to have what you want, until you learn to follow orders."

He pulled her to her feet and leaned down, his lips brushing hers. "You going to do what I say, baby?"

"No." More excitement filled her veins, like the sweetest drug. Fighting with this man excited her like nothing else.

He leaned down, picked her up, and tossed her over his shoulder. His palm smacked against her ass.

As she gasped, he strode into the bedroom and everything tumbled as he dropped her on the bed. The bedside lamp clicked on and he stood over her—big and imposing. He shrugged his shoulder harness off and dropped it on a chair. Then he started unbuttoning his shirt with slow, methodical movements.

Darcy licked her lips. Each button that loosened, showcasing a widening sliver of bronze skin, made her breath hitch. Then the shirt was open and he slipped it off.

Oh, boy. She drank in the hard chest, the defined abs, and the tiny smattering of dark hair across his pecs. She wanted to lick him—every ridge, every dip, every sleek line of muscle.

"Take the dress off," he ordered.

That dark voice, filled with authority, shivered over her. "No."

He leaned over her, gripping her chin with his fingers. His thumb brushed her lips. "So defiant."

Then his hands slid down. He caught the neckline of her dress and pulled it lower. Her shoulders were already bare and, as the fabric slid downward, the tops of her breasts were on view. The satin caught on the tips of her breasts, and she was excruciatingly conscious that she wasn't wearing a bra. There'd been no way to wear one in this dress. He gave a sharp tug.

The fabric pooled around her waist, leaving her breasts bare.

His gaze was on her and he made a hungry sound. She felt her nipples pebble.

Alastair placed one knee on the bed, leaned over, and closed his lips around one nipple. He sucked hard, and she cried out.

She pushed up into his mouth, not fighting him now. *Oh, Jesus.* It was so good.

He switched to the other breast, one hand sliding under her and lifting her to his busy mouth. Darcy slid her hands into his hair, tugging hard. Desire was a molten fire in her belly and her panties were saturated.

He nipped at the lower curve of her breast. "Take the dress off."

"Make me." She hardly recognized her husky voice.

Alastair pulled back, hands reaching for her ankles. His hands circled her, then his fingers slid upward. Higher. Over her calves, her knees. Higher. Sliding along her thighs, pushing her dress higher.

Their gazes locked and the hunger she saw burning in his eyes, etched on his rugged face, made her chest tight. She couldn't breathe, she was burning up.

He bunched her dress higher, baring her thighs.

"You going to do what I say?" he growled.

"Why should I?" Her resistance was slipping. She

wanted him to touch her more than she wanted anything else.

"Because if you do, then I'll fuck you so hard you'll be hoarse from screaming my name as you come."

Her belly spasmed. Never in a million years would she have guessed that Alastair Burke would be a dirty talker in bed. It turned her on like crazy. She lifted her hips and he smiled, anticipation flaring. He sank his hands in the dress and pulled it down her legs.

She leaned back on the bed, wearing only a tiny pair of black lace panties that revealed more than they covered.

His gaze ran over her. "You are so damn gorgeous, Darcy Aphrodite Ward."

For the first time in her life, she thought her full name sounded beautiful.

His head lowered, and he pressed a hard kiss to her lips, his tongue sliding against hers. Then she lost his mouth as it moved lower—down her neck, between her breasts, down her belly. His stubble scraped her skin, and she couldn't stop the shocked little cries that escaped her lips.

Then, he pressed a kiss to her hipbone and she quivered.

"You want my mouth, baby?"

"Yes. Yes."

"My tongue?"

Another spasm in her belly. "Alastair."

"Damn, I love hearing my name on your lips." He gripped her waist and flipped her over, onto her belly.

No. "Alastair, I—"

He gave one cheek a quick slap. "You take what I give you, Darcy. All of it." Then his hands were caressing her, kneading the skin of her ass.

She let out a small moan.

"I thought I'd lost you tonight. After you went over that railing..."

His voice cut off and she pushed against him. "I'm right here, honey. All yours."

"Yes, you are." He gripped her hips, nudging her closer to the headboard. "Grip the slats, Darcy. Hard."

He lifted her up onto her hands and knees, and with butterflies bursting in her belly, she quickly followed orders. She wrapped her fingers tight around the wooden slats on his headboard.

"Fuck, you're gorgeous." His hands slid beneath the lace, stroking her.

She pushed back against him, desperate. His fingers stroking through her damp folds felt so good. "Please."

His hand twisted and he tore her panties off. "I'm so hard, Darcy, and it's all your fault." He stroked her folds again. "Spread your knees."

She did instantly, with no thought to disobeying. No one had ever wanted her like this. So all-consuming and desperate. No one had ever wanted her like Alastair did.

"Now she follows orders." He pumped a finger inside her.

Her hands tightened on the headboard. *Yes.*

"Fucking tight. Just waiting for my cock."

Alastair's frank words were winding her higher. She'd never felt desire like this, so hot, so on edge. She might not survive.

He worked a second finger inside her. "This is mine, isn't it?"

He added another finger, stretching her. She moaned.

"It's been mine for a while."

"Alastair." She pushed back against him. "More. I need—"

"I know what you need."

Then she felt his hot breath on her thighs. He nudged her legs wider apart and his mouth was on her.

Darcy cried out. Alastair Burke's mouth was between her legs. His tongue lapped at her and her entire body trembled. *God. God.*

His tongue was inside her, working her. She tried to stop the sounds escaping from her throat, but then his talented mouth found her clit.

Her cries turned loud and desperate, her body shaking. "Alastair."

"Come, Darcy," he growled against her.

Her orgasm hit hard and her vision wavered. Wave after wave of pleasure swamped her, and she didn't care who heard her cry out Alastair's name.

CHAPTER TWELVE

Alastair's jaw was tight from gritting his teeth. His need for Darcy was huge, pumping inside him.

He felt sensations clamp down on the base of his spine and his cock ached. He'd never needed anything like this. Never needed anyone the way he needed Darcy.

Her hands were loosely holding onto the headboard. That sexy, naked body was limp and flushed. Damn, that ass. Her delicious taste was still on his tongue.

He reached over to the bedside table and grabbed a foil packet. He tore it open with his teeth, and made short work of rolling the condom on. Then, he gripped Darcy's waist, pulled her up, and turned her. He wanted to see her face when he slid inside her.

Her eyelids fluttered. So damn beautiful.

They faced each other on their knees. He knew that this woman had brought him to his knees a long time ago.

He'd tried to fight it, but every interaction had tangled her with him more and more.

Alastair slid his hand between her slim thighs and stroked. She let out a keening moan. He thrust a finger inside her. "Mine. This is mine."

She bit her lip.

"Darcy, tell me."

"Yes, yours, Alastair. Now fuck me, please."

He circled her waist and lifted her. She gasped. He could tell that she liked that he could lift her so easily.

He pressed her back to the headboard, and gripped his cock with one hand, lodging the head between her slick folds.

"Look at me," he growled.

Blue-gray eyes met his, and then he slammed her down on his cock.

She cried out.

Fuck. Jesus. She felt so good. Hot, slick, tight. Her fingers dug into his shoulders and her head fell back.

"God, yes." She wrapped her legs around him.

As he lifted her up, she drove herself back down, letting out a wild moan.

"You feel so good, Darcy." He worked himself inside her, sinking deep.

"Alastair—"

"I love being buried deep in your sweetness."

She gripped his shoulders, bouncing up and down, taking his cock and meeting each one of his driving thrusts.

"Darcy." He grunted, the pleasure growing inside

him. He reached up, tugging her hair to make her look at him. "Look at me when you come."

"Okay." Her nails bit into his skin and her heels dug into his ass.

"I can feel you trembling around me."

She cried out, her head falling back, and she started coming.

Alastair thrust into her, and then lodged himself deep, staying there. He yanked her closer and sank his teeth into the spot where her shoulder met her neck. She cried out again, and his orgasm slammed into him, ripping a groan from his throat.

He knelt there, chest heaving, sensations still rushing through him. Darcy dropped her forehead to his, her arms and legs still wrapped around him.

"Okay?" His voice was hoarse.

"Better than okay." She lifted her head and smiled. Her cheeks were filled with color. "That was *fabulous*."

Warmth filled his chest. After he lowered her to the bed, he kissed her, nipping her bottom lip.

Her eyelids fluttered. "We might kill each other if we have sex like that every time, but it'll be fantastic."

Alastair moved lower, brushing his teeth along her jaw, down her neck, across her collarbone. He took it slow, savoring her. She stretched under him, making a sound close to a purr.

Darcy Ward was beneath him, wet from taking his cock, and she was perfect.

He spotted the bruise forming where he'd bitten her and he pressed a kiss to the mark. His mark. She looked up at him, her eyes huge.

Shit. Darcy was more than just a distraction, she was taking over his life. He felt a pressure in his chest.

"I'm hungry," she murmured.

"I'll feed you. So you have enough energy for me to fuck you again."

As he pushed off the bed, Darcy rose up on her elbow. She didn't bother to hide the fact that she was checking out his naked body. After a quick stop to the bathroom to deal with the condom, he headed for the kitchen.

After checking his phone—no messages or updates—he raided his cupboard and refrigerator, and grabbed some cheese and crackers. When he got back to his bedroom, Darcy was wrapped in a sheet. He set the plate down on the bed.

She smiled. "You should be naked all the time." Her nose wrinkled. "Except you look pretty darn fine in a suit."

"Really?"

"I may or may not have had inappropriate thoughts of taking your suit off in the past." She grabbed a slice of cheese and nibbled.

Darcy was in his bed. He felt pretty damn satisfied about that.

Then her face changed. "I wonder what the Collector is doing?" she said quietly.

"He'd better be enjoying his last night of freedom."

She was quiet for a minute. "I realize now that taking down Silk Road is very personal for you."

He turned his head, looking at the framed picture of him and his mom. "Yeah. Losing my mother...it was why

I joined the FBI, and why I helped create a team specializing in art and antiquities crime. I want justice for her."

"I always knew something deeper was driving you." Darcy stroked his arm. "What happened to you after she died?"

"Foster homes. My father was never in the picture." Alastair chewed on a cracker. "It took me a while to settle. I had terrible nightmares for years. Every night, remembering her screams, that I was helpless to get to her."

Darcy's hand slid into his and tightened. "You were a child. There was nothing you could have done."

He looked at her slim, competent fingers. He'd never held hands with a woman before. "My mom had nothing, came from nothing. She'd run away from a bad home as a teenager. But she worked hard. She was a waitress." Alastair smiled, remembering his mother's pretty face, the affection in her eyes. "She wanted me to have a job where I got to wear a suit." He'd forgotten that. He'd forgotten so many of the good times in his focus on finding revenge. "She always thought people in suits had important jobs."

"She loved you."

"Yes, she did."

Darcy shifted, climbing onto his lap. He wrapped his arms around her, absorbing her warmth.

"I bet your mom would love to know that you look mighty fine in a suit, Alastair." She lowered her head, pressing a kiss to his shoulder. "And pretty darn good without one, as well."

He barked out a laugh.

"She'd be proud of the important job you do."

And as Darcy kept nibbling on his skin, he looked down at her dark head. He felt the need growing in him again. "What are you doing?"

She looked up at him, then nudged him. He fell on his back and Darcy straddled him.

"This time, I'm going to fuck you, Special Agent Burke."

"Really?" Need slammed into him.

"And remember I told you that you'd owe me if I got those impossible, undetectable trackers for you?"

Her smile made his gut clench. "Yes."

"Time to pay up." She smiled. "Now, where are your handcuffs?"

DARCY RACED into the living room, looking for her shoes. Early-morning sex had left her feeling tremendous, but running late.

"My shoes?"

"Next to the front door."

She looked up. Alastair was in the kitchen, dressed in a crisp shirt and trousers, hair damp from the shower. Memories of the shower slammed back into her. He'd pinned her to the tiles, whispered dirty things in her ear, and given her another soul-shattering orgasm. And just as delicious was the memory of him stretched out beneath her with his hands cuffed to his headboard, muscles straining as she'd touched him. *Mmm.*

She stared at him now. He was wearing his shoulder holster over his shirt, and damn, he looked sexy. Her exhausted and satiated body still reacted to the sight of him.

"You are so damn handsome," she said.

He shot her a half smile and mixed the eggs he was cooking.

God, Darcy knew his mom would be so proud of him. "What are you cooking for me?" She slipped on her heels and made her way over to him.

"Scrambled eggs." He slid a plate across the island toward her.

Suddenly ravenous, Darcy sat and ate. It was pretty handy having a guy who could cook. "Any news on the search warrant?"

"I spoke to Thom while you were in the bathroom. He said we should have it soon."

Darcy heard something in his voice and studied him. He was filled with a fine tension, visible in the line of his shoulders and his posture.

She knew he'd been in contact with the onsite teams during the night and morning. "The diamonds haven't moved, and no one's been in or out of the penthouse."

"Correct."

God, she hoped no one had cut the diamonds up overnight. The Louvre and the Dashwood would be beyond pissed.

"And you really think the Collector will be there?" she asked.

"Yeah. I'm guessing they're waiting for the Collector to arrive today."

She lifted her chin. "We're going to get them."

Intense green eyes met hers. "We are."

They finished up their breakfast and got ready. Darcy swiped on some lipstick. She was wearing black, fitted trousers, and a white shirt. She added a chunky green bangle at her wrist. Just because they were taking down international black-market thieves didn't mean she couldn't look good while they did it.

She glanced at Alastair's phone. It hadn't rung yet.

Then she started pacing. The minutes ticked by, and still no call about the search warrant.

"Waiting sucks."

Alastair opened his laptop, leaning against the counter as he touched the keyboard. "When you work for the government, you learn to have some patience."

She wrinkled her nose. "I prefer action."

He snorted. "I'd noticed. And caffeine."

She smiled at him. He really did look too damn handsome. Even though he was obviously on edge and alert waiting for the search warrant, for the first time since she'd known him, his face didn't have its usual harsh intensity. It looked relaxed. She guessed that out-of-this-world, wild sex would probably do that.

"What's that smile for?" He was staring at her face.

"Oh, just thinking about how good you are in bed."

He cocked his head.

She lifted a hand, rubbing her thumb over her lips. "How good you are with your hands and mouth. How impressive your—" when he raised a brow at her, she grinned "—stamina is."

Suddenly, he pushed away from the counter and stalked toward her.

The intensity was back in his green eyes. Excitement

shivered through her, and she backed up until she hit the back of the couch.

"Alastair—" God, that look in his eyes…

He reached her, gripped her hips, and spun her around. Her hips hit the back of the couch.

Then he leaned down, his lips teasing her ear. "I'm going to fuck you, Darcy. Right here."

All the air shuddered out of her. He bent her over the couch, his fingers working the zipper of her trousers. A second later, he pushed them down, along with her panties.

Then his fingers were between her legs, stroking. She bit down to stifle a moan.

"Wet for me already, Ms. Ward. Naughty."

"I'm always ready for you." She rode his hand, needing him to touch her.

"All those times we talked, fought, argued…were you wet for me?" His fingers thrust deep.

She cried out, pleasure spiraling through her.

"Answer me," he growled.

"Yes. God, yes."

Then she heard the sound of a zipper lowering, the crinkle of foil, and then he thrust forward, filling her.

Darcy moaned.

"Tilt your hips, baby. Take more."

She did and he pumped deep. She gripped the couch for dear life and bit her lip. Sensations rocketed through her.

"God, Darcy—" His voice was a growl.

She could hear his control breaking. Watching, listening, and feeling Alastair Burke lose control was her new favorite thing.

"More, Alastair. Don't stop."

"I never want to stop. I want to stay right here inside you forever."

His hand slid around and cupped her chin, tilting her head to the side. Their gazes met, and his mouth covered hers—the kiss hard and demanding, like the way he was taking her body.

Then his other hand slipped down over her belly. His fingers found her clit and rolled it.

"Come." He thrust hard inside her.

It was an order and she wasn't going to disobey it. Her release exploded through her and she screamed.

Alastair pumped again—once, twice, three times. He lodged his cock deep and groaned through his own orgasm.

When Darcy blinked her eyes open, all she could hear was their harsh breathing.

"Wow," she murmured.

He leaned down and kissed her shoulder. Then, there was the sudden ringing of a phone. She waited for Alastair to pull away, but instead, she felt him reach into his pocket. Darcy went to move, but he pressed his other hand between her shoulder blades, holding her in place.

"Thom?"

Oh, God. He was talking to Thom while he was still *inside* her. She shoved back, but Alastair kept her pinned in place.

"Got it. Yeah, Darcy's right here." The hand on her back slid down and around, then between her legs. He tweaked her swollen clit again. She glared at him over her shoulder, but as pleasure hit her, she bit her lip.

"You tracked down Elettaria Inc." He made a humming sound. "A bunch of dummy corporations." His gaze met Darcy's. "But elettaria is a genus of plant. *Elettaria cardamomum* is the true name for cardamom."

Darcy gasped. "And cardamom was one of the main spices sold along the historical Silk Road."

"Yeah, we're on our way." Alastair shifted his hips, his fingers rubbing her clit.

The move sent a wave of latent pleasure through her and she moaned.

"See you soon, Thom."

"You are incorrigible." She shoved against Alastair.

He kept working her clit.

"Alastair!" The sensations were building again, her belly on fire.

He didn't let up. Not until she moaned his name through another short, sharp orgasm. Then he pulled out of her, and pressed a hard kiss to her lips.

"We got the warrant."

Excitement shivered through her. "Luckily I'm feeling too good to be angry with you about that stunt. Let me clean up and then let's go."

He nodded. "It's time to end this, and take down the Collector."

"Then let's do it."

CHAPTER THIRTEEN

Alastair pulled his car to a stop at the Adana Tower and climbed out.

Darcy leaped out of the car, bursting with energy. As they headed toward the group of agents and the THS gang waiting near the entrance, he wanted to grab her hand, but he restrained himself. Barely.

After touching her all night, he wanted to keep doing it. He didn't want to stop.

She looked at him and clearly read him like an open book. A sexy smile curved her lips. "Behave."

As they neared the group, Thom, Dec, and Cal looked up.

"No one came out of the penthouse all night." Thom handed over some paperwork.

Alastair scanned the warrant.

"Someone did enter this morning," Thom said.

Alastair lifted his head.

"Older gentleman. He's one of the founding members of Cochran, Dean, and Porter."

"Lawyer," Alastair said.

Darcy leaned forward. "You think he's the Collector?"

"Let's find out," Alastair said. "Time to pay a visit."

"We're having that discussion about my sister," Dec said. "Soon."

Cal's gaze narrowed, his voice was low. "I say we just beat him up."

"I can't hear everything you're saying," Darcy said, from the other side of Alastair. "But I'm pretty sure I don't like it."

"You see that freaking hickey on your neck?" Dec growled.

Darcy's gaze narrowed. "Do I ask you about your sex life?"

Cal groaned. "Don't use the word sex. Sisters are not allowed to say it to their brothers."

Darcy rounded on her brother.

Alastair gripped her arm. "Can we take down Silk Road first, then continue this?"

Dec and Cal both straightened. Darcy nodded. Once again, Alastair was glad he was an only child.

Alastair waved at the group of armed agents. As they moved toward the front doors of the Adana Tower, Darcy did as well.

He scowled at her and opened his mouth.

"I've earned this." Her gaze narrowed. "And you know it."

Alastair sucked in a breath. "Fine. But you stay back."

They headed through the lobby and over to the elevators. Thom had already briefed the building's security. It was a tense ride up to the penthouse level.

The elevator opened into a small lobby covered in expensive marble and a large, carved wooden door. He nodded at Thom, and his partner knocked on the door.

It opened, and a handsome young man stood there, wearing a tailored suit. His tousled blond hair was styled, and he was cradling a mug of coffee like he didn't have a care in the world.

"We have a warrant to search the premises." Alastair held out the paperwork.

The man's face moved into a concerned look. "I see, Mr....?"

"Special Agent Burke. FBI."

"Ah."

An older man appeared at the man's back. The young man turned and handed the paperwork over to him.

"I'll let my lawyer take a look at it."

Smug bastard. He reeked of privilege and superiority. Alastair had met many wealthy people in his career. Most of them were damn hard-working business owners and philanthropists. But there was always an elite asshole lurking around a corner in DC.

The younger man smiled and it rubbed Alastair the wrong way.

Suddenly, Darcy pushed forward, and Alastair barely resisted rolling his eyes. He threw out an arm to stop her.

"Wait," she said. "I know you."

The man tilted his head, and his smile widened,

showing lots of perfect teeth. "I'm sure I'd remember a woman as lovely as you."

Alastair scowled and stepped closer to her.

"You were in the Dashwood. The morning we stopped those kids trying to steal the sculpture."

The man gave a negligent shrug. "I often visit all of DC's venerable institutions."

"Name," Alastair demanded.

That smug smile stayed in place. "William Henry Acton."

Now it was Declan who muscled forward. Darcy gasped.

Alastair frowned at the siblings. He was missing something. "That mean something to you?"

"Back in the seventies," Dec said. "In Ecuador, when our parents first met—"

"There was an English treasure hunter named Henry Acton." Darcy glared at the blond man. "He tried to steal a priceless Incan emerald my parents were searching for. He tried to murder them."

William just smiled. "My grandfather was a true adventurer and visionary."

"He didn't die in Ecuador?" Darcy asked.

William continued smiling, but something nasty moved through his blue gaze. "Your parents pushed him off a cliff into a caiman-infested river."

"To save their own lives," Darcy spat.

Suddenly, the lawyer stepped back into view. He gave William a small nod. Alastair waved to his team and they moved forward to begin searching the penthouse.

Alastair strode past Acton, keeping Darcy close. As his agents spread out, he watched Darcy lift her tablet.

Then she gasped.

"What?" he asked.

"The diamonds are moving. *Downward.*"

William Acton's smile slipped. Clearly no one had found the trackers. *Surprise, asshole.*

"Thom!" Alastair followed Darcy.

She swiveled, moving through the penthouse. She burst through a door and into a study. It was done in dark wood, burgundy leather, and covered in bookshelves. She stopped in front of one of the fully-loaded shelves.

"Here," she said.

Alastair reached out, moving his hands over the shelves.

"There must be something behind it," she said. "We need to find the mechanism to open it."

Darcy and Thom joined him, all of them looking. Suddenly, Darcy touched something, and Alastair heard a *click.*

Part of the bookshelf opened, moving away from the wall. Alastair gripped it and swung it wide.

The silver doors of an elevator were behind it.

"It wasn't on any schematics," Thom said.

Alastair cursed and strode out of the study. He looked at Acton, and the young man was smirking again.

Alastair didn't waste any time with the asshole. "Someone arrest him!"

He strode out, barking orders as they all entered the main elevator.

"Someone contact the agents on the street. No vehicles leave here. No one leaves the building. I want every door, window, and trash chute secured."

Darcy tapped on her tablet. "Diamonds are still moving. They're outside! North side."

The elevator slowed and the doors opened. They jogged through the lobby and out into the sunshine.

Agents swarmed them. "No one's left, Agent Burke."

"The diamonds are outside. Find them!"

They circled around the building and Thom suddenly pointed upward. "Look."

Alastair spotted a broken window on the second level.

A second later, there was a squeal of tires. They all turned, and down the street, a black Mercedes peeled away from the curb.

"Fuck!" he roared.

All of a sudden, a car screeched to a halt beside him. His car. The door opened and he saw Darcy behind the wheel.

"Get in."

He leaped into the passenger seat, and before he'd even closed the door, she careened out onto the road. He quickly pulled on his seatbelt.

"Here." She shoved her tablet at him.

Darcy followed the Mercedes, driving like a race car driver hyped up on caffeine. A few times, he had to brace his hand on the roof.

"Darcy—"

"Don't worry, Dec and Cal taught me to drive."

"Fuck," he muttered.

She smiled at him, and despite the circumstances, he

was struck by how beautiful she was. Suddenly, it hit him that he was falling for her. All the way, completely. His chest contracted.

He knew that it hurt to care, to love, and then to lose. He'd avoided it ever since he'd lost his mom. He'd probably be terrible at it since his experience was limited.

Darcy spun the wheel, taking a corner way too fast.

"Don't kill us," he said.

"I'll do my best."

He growled. "I want you safe."

"And I'm never going to follow your orders, Alastair."

That was probably the truth. "Except in bed."

She winked at him. "When it suits me."

God, she was something. The Mercedes had pulled ahead, and Alastair could just see it in the distance. Then he checked the side mirror and tensed.

"Darcy."

"Yeah."

"There's a sedan coming up behind us. Coming in fast."

She looked in the rearview mirror, her eyes widening. "He's speeding up. He's going to—"

The sedan rammed into the back of them with a crunch of metal. Darcy clamped her hands on the wheel, trying to keep hold of it.

"Hang on!" She pressed her foot down.

Their vehicle shot forward and Alastair gripped the door handle. She fish-tailed across the thankfully empty road, took a corner way too fast, but she managed to put some distance between them and the sedan.

She looked in the mirror. "They're still coming!"

Alastair pulled his Glock out and lowered the window. He unclipped his belt.

"Alastair, no—"

He reached out the window, aimed, and took the shot. An answering hail of bullets hit the back window, shattering it.

Darcy ducked down with a short scream. "Shit. Shit."

"Hold us steady." Alastair pulled himself half out of the window and fired again.

"Alastair! Get back in here."

He hit one of the approaching car's tires, sending the vehicle careening out of control. It went up on the sidewalk and hit a fire hydrant.

He slid back into his seat.

"I want you safe, too." She slapped at his chest. "Don't do that again."

"I'm fine."

Ahead, the Potomac appeared in their field of view. In the distance, the Mercedes turned.

"There." Alastair pointed. "He's headed for that marina."

Darcy slowed. "It's a yacht club."

The river was wider here, and several docks poked out toward the middle of the river. They were lined with yachts of all different sizes.

When she pulled into the parking lot, Alastair spotted the abandoned Mercedes.

"What now?" she asked.

"Wait for backup, and then we search the marina." He tapped the tablet. "I've sent Thom our location."

Darcy peered out the windshield. Then she tensed. "Alastair, look."

A large superyacht was docked at the end of one of the rows. Several uniformed crewmembers were scrambling about the deck, pulling in ropes.

Readying the ship to leave.

Dammit. That had to belong to the Collector.

Alastair opened the glove compartment and pulled out spare ammunition. "You wait here for our backup. Tell Thom where I am." Then he leaned across the car, slid a hand behind Darcy's head, and pressed a hard kiss to her lips.

"No." She gripped his wrist. "You should wait."

"I'm not going to let them get away." He opened his door.

"The Collector has to be Henry Acton. Dad was sure he died in Ecuador, but he must have survived."

"I'm going in to find him, get the diamonds, and end this."

Fear skittered over her face. "Please wait."

Alastair wavered. He wanted to ease her fear...but he'd started this journey a long time ago. He had to finish it. He straightened. For his mom.

"Tell Thom, and stay safe."

Something flickered in Darcy's gaze, something that made his gut churn.

"Alastair, stay."

"I can't." He pressed another quick, desperate kiss to her lips, then he slid out of the car. He was doing this for her too. "They won't hurt anyone I love again."

Time to get justice for his mother, and for every time Silk Road had tried to harm Darcy.

DARCY STOOD by the car staring at the super yacht. It had several levels, some with decks at the back, and a bridge at the top, covered in fancy-looking antennas.

Alastair had left her.

She let out a shuddering breath. She felt hollow and alone. Discarded.

He'd slipped aboard moments ago. She wrapped her arms around her middle. When the hell were Thom and her brothers going to arrive?

Alastair had rushed in there, with no care for his own safety. She bit her lip. God, she didn't know she could hurt this much. After the way he'd touched her last night, possessed her, she'd thought she'd found that once-in-a-lifetime connection.

But he'd left her.

Can you blame him? If her parents had been killed by Silk Road, she'd stop at nothing to bring the group to justice.

She swallowed. *They won't hurt anyone I love again.*

She froze. In her head, she pictured the look on his face as he'd made love to her during the night—the hunger, the desperation, the absorption. She felt the way he touched, like every caress mattered.

They won't hurt anyone I love again. Did he mean more than just his mother?

Oh, God. She pushed away from the car. It didn't

matter. She was falling for the hard-headed, bossy man, and she'd realized something in the last few days. Being in love wasn't about someone sweeping you off your feet, or them always showing you grand gestures. It went both ways. It was taking care of each other, ensuring that the other person was okay, giving them what they needed. It was the small things as well.

Then she heard gunshots.

Her stomach clenched. Alastair was in trouble.

She took a step forward. Who knew how many Silk Road thugs were on the yacht? She scanned the parking lot. She couldn't wait any longer. Alastair needed help.

Darcy snatched up her tablet and slipped it into her pocket. She wished she had a weapon, but that still wasn't going to stop her.

She jogged down the floating walkway toward the yacht. There were no crewmembers or guards in sight. She raced up the ramp.

Two suited guards were unconscious, zip-tied and lying on the ground. She grinned. Damn, her man was good.

She snuck through the first door she found and paused. *Wow*. It was all glossy, tan wood, cream leather, and gold fixtures. Expensive-looking, but a little gaudy for her tastes.

She lifted the tablet and pulled up the tracking map. The diamonds were toward the back of the ship. She slipped through the hallway. It was lined with wooden doors, but they were all closed.

At the end of the hall, there was another door, with a glass panel in the center. She pressed to the side of the hallway and moved closer. The murmur of voices rumbled through the door. Then she craned her head, peeking through the glass.

Bile rose in her throat. It was some sort of open living area and it was filled with armed guards. Alastair was sitting in the center of the space, tied to a chair.

Oh, no.

"The Collector will be here soon," a man said.

It had to be Henry Acton.

She peeked in again and saw the diamond case resting on a table. She had to get Alastair free, get the diamonds, and get out of there until their backup arrived.

Easy. No sweat.

As she watched, one guard reached back and punched Alastair in the face. His head whipped to the side, blood on his mouth. She bit her lip to stifle her cry.

She ducked back down. She wanted to rush in there, but that wouldn't help. *Think, Darcy, think.* She pulled out her tablet. She needed to use the skills she had. She looked around and spotted a small, covered, electrical panel on the wall. It took her a second to remove the plate. She lifted her tablet, plugged in, and got into the yacht's controls. She smiled grimly. She was now on their wireless system.

Okay. Now what? She tapped, hacking into the lighting and ventilation system. It wasn't much, but it was something.

She turned the lights off in the room. Instantly, voices rose in alarm. Then, she started blinking the lights on and off.

Now, commotion broke out inside. She peeked

through the glass again. Alastair was on his feet, still tied to the chair, but swinging it around and kicking his attackers. He banged into one guard, then kicked another one into the wall.

Darcy opened the door. She slid inside, staying close to the wall. She circled the room, moving over to a built-in bar. She ducked behind it and opened a drawer. She fished around and pulled out a knife.

Then she turned. There was a guard with his back to her.

She crept closer. Suddenly, he turned and spotted her.

Gripping the hilt of the knife tighter, she launched herself at him. She stabbed at him, but he dodged the blow.

From her vantage point, she had a direct view of Alastair. She watched as a guard rammed a punch into Alastair's gut, sending him lurching backward.

"Out of my way," she snapped at the guard. Alastair needed her.

She stabbed again, and this time, she caught the man on the side. He slammed into the bar, tripped, and cracked his head on the edge of the bar. He went down hard.

She spun and found Alastair standing in the center of the room, his chest heaving. The other guards were all on the floor around him, groaning.

She lifted her tablet and turned the flashing lights off.

Green eyes locked on her. "I told you to stay in the car."

"Surprise." She walked over to him. "No way I was

letting you hog all the action." She pressed her lips to his. "Or get hurt."

"You drive me crazy."

"And you love it."

"Yeah, I do."

Their gazes locked and, for a second, Darcy couldn't breathe.

"You going to cut these ropes off?"

She blinked. *Ropes, right.* "Turn around."

He spun, and she used the knife to saw through the rope. The chair dropped to the floor, and Alastair yanked the ropes off.

Then he grabbed her, pulled her off her feet, and yanked her in for a kiss.

"Let's get the diamonds," he said. "Then find Thom and the others."

They turned to the table...and Darcy's heart sank.

The diamond case was gone.

Suddenly, she heard a steady *thwap thwap* sound coming from outside. A helicopter swept overhead.

"Shit," Alastair muttered. "It's coming in to land on the top deck."

"The Collector!"

CHAPTER FOURTEEN

A lastair stayed close to Darcy as they pushed down the paneled hall. "Can you turn the lights off across the ship?"

She smiled. "Can you take down multiple bad guys like a badass?"

Alastair stared at her. Bright, smart, sexy Darcy. His heart thudded in his chest. No question now, he was falling in love, and hell, he was right near the bottom of the fall.

He wanted to haul her close, but right now, he needed to get the diamonds, catch the Collector, and most importantly, keep Darcy safe.

He'd do anything to keep her safe.

She tapped on her tablet and the lights went out. In the near darkness, they slid their hands along the walls until they reached a set of stairs. They moved up. He slowed near the top, squinting into the dimness, ready for anything.

That's when Alastair's ankle hit something.

Trip wire. *Shit.*

He spun and threw himself over Darcy.

The grenade went off, but there was no shrapnel. Instead, gas filled the air. Darcy coughed.

"Drop low." He pulled her down, but he was already feeling sluggish.

Darcy went limp, collapsing beneath him. *No, dammit.* Alastair dropped heavily to his knees, pulling her close and holding her tight. Every muscle in his body tensed. He couldn't fail her.

He looked up and coughed, spotting dark shapes moving through the gas.

Black crept in around the edges of his vision. He fought it, but a second later, he lost consciousness.

When Alastair came to, he was slumped in a chair, his hands handcuffed behind him.

The lights were back on and Darcy was lying on the plush carpet in front of him. Fear burned through him, and he stared at her, hoping against hope that she was okay. He saw the gentle rise and fall of her chest. She was breathing. *Thank God.*

Then, he looked up.

They were in a dining room. One wall consisted of floor-to-ceiling glass, leading out onto a wide deck. Guards in body armor, holding rifles, lined the outer perimeter of the space. They looked military-trained.

He took note of the diamond case resting on the table.

"Where's the Collector?" he said.

No one moved or spoke. Then, he heard the click of

heels on the wooden floor. He expected to see an aging Henry Acton. Instead, an elegant woman in her fifties entered the room. She wore a stylish, navy-blue pantsuit, her carefully-colored blonde hair was swept up in a neat style, and the discreet work she'd clearly had done left her face unlined.

"You look surprised, Agent Burke." She smiled. She had a cultured British accent. "I assume you were expecting my father."

"Henry Acton was your father."

As she nodded, large diamonds winked from her earlobes. "Brian, bring me some tea, please."

One of the soldiers moved over to the kitchenette.

"So that makes the asshole at the Adana your son," Alastair said.

The woman's faint smile didn't waver. "Correct. My lawyers are working to get him released from FBI custody as we speak."

"You're all going down," Alastair said. "William will be locked away for a very long time, Mrs....?"

"*Ms.* Diana Acton. I married, but kept my father's name in his honor."

She accepted a cup of tea from her guard. She took a moment to squeeze some lemon in, then sipped.

"I've been running Silk Road for decades, Agent Burke. I had partners for a time, but it was me building it, one step at a time. My private collection is vast."

"Your collection of stolen goods is vast. And you're a murderer."

Her blue eyes flashed. "My father was murdered. He died in a fucking jungle like trash."

Now Alastair heard the edge in her voice. He was getting to her.

"From what I've heard, he was a killer and a thief." Darcy's voice.

Alastair glanced down and saw she was sitting up. She looked pale, but she was conscious.

"He tried to kill my parents," Darcy continued. "He killed a man helping them."

Diana Acton's gaze narrowed on Darcy. "They *killed* him. I worshiped my father. He was a great man."

Darcy snorted.

The older woman's smile changed, sharpened. "It doesn't matter. I'll soon have my revenge—on your parents, on Treasure Hunter Security—" she looked at Alastair "—and on everyone who thought they could stop me and Silk Road."

Alastair felt a chill go down his spine. "What are you talking about?"

"Well, Agent Burke, my collection contains an impressive group of artifacts with certain...powers."

His gut hardened.

"Abilities I can use to make Silk Road a force to be reckoned with across the world. Governments will fall over themselves to please me."

Shit. Alastair knew that there were artifacts that existed that needed to be locked away. That couldn't be left in the wrong hands. He needed to warn Team 52.

"Now, let's see what we have here?" Diana drawled.

The woman picked up the diamond case and flicked the lid open. Pleasure suffused her face.

"Oh, yes." The words came out as a sigh. "I can use these to control others."

"These aren't pieces of ancient lost technology." Darcy rolled her eyes. "You're buying into your own sense of grandeur. They're just diamonds."

"There are too many legends attached to these jewels." A muscle ticked in Diana's jaw. "My researchers assured me that they *must* contain certain powers."

Alastair kept his gaze on Diana. The woman wasn't thinking straight. Her lust for power had warped her. "We'll stop you."

"Really?" Diana shook her head. "You and Ms. Ward will be at the bottom of the ocean in a few hours. No one will ever find your bodies."

Alastair felt the flare of vibrations through the floor. Damn, the yacht's engines. The ship was moving. *Fuck.*

His team would arrive to an empty dock.

"And now, I'm going to teach you both a lesson." Diana nodded her head.

Two guards grabbed Darcy and dragged her forward.

"Let me go!"

Alastair rose, yanking against his handcuffs. Another guard moved, shoving him back down into the chair.

Helpless, he watched as Darcy was dragged to one of the tables. The two guards lifted her onto the surface, even as she twisted and fought. They pinned her down on her back.

Diana walked closer, heels clicking. She pulled out a small bundle and unrolled it.

Alastair's gut cramped. It was a toolset.

The Silk Road man who'd hurt his mother had carried the same bundle.

It was the kind carried by torturers.

"Maybe I won't throw your body into the ocean, Ms. Ward. Perhaps I'll throw your broken body somewhere where it can be a lesson to your parents, Treasure Hunter Security, the FBI, and, most especially, to him." She pointed at Alastair.

Alastair tugged against the handcuffs. *No.*

"I believe you've seen something like this before, Agent Burke." Diana's smile was mean. "When your mother died."

Every muscle in his body locked. *No. Not again.*

"LET ME GO!" Darcy heaved up, trying to break free.

She struggled against the guards holding her down. She got a leg free and kicked one man in the stomach.

His hand flashed out and slapped her face.

Ow. She saw stars. From across the room, she heard Alastair growl. The men pinned her arms flush against her sides, fingers biting into her biceps and ankles to hold her in place.

Diana Acton stepped into view. The woman held a large set of pliers in one hand and a small knife in the other

Oh, God. Darcy's stomach revolted.

"Do I start with your teeth or your lovely skin, Ms. Ward?"

Darcy glared at the woman. "I vote neither."

The woman shook her head. Then she set the pliers down and started slicing the buttons off Darcy's shirt. The buttons made a pinging sound as they hit the floor.

Damn. Fear was like acid in Darcy's veins.

Diana pushed Darcy's shirt open, baring her skin and pretty, pale-green bra. Then the woman pressed the knife just below Darcy's breasts.

She moved the blade downward.

Darcy hissed at the sting and heard Alastair curse wildly. The cut wasn't too deep and she gritted her teeth. She was not giving this bitch the satisfaction of hearing her make a noise. Blood welled on her belly.

Diana nodded, like she was approving her own handiwork. Then she lifted the knife again, and stroked once more down Darcy's stomach.

This cut was deeper and hurt more. Darcy choked back her cry.

On the third cut, Darcy turned her head, struggling not to make a sound. Her gaze locked with Alastair's.

Oh, he was barely holding on. Emotion filled her chest. His big body was tense, straining forward against the cuffs holding him. His face was sheened with perspiration.

She didn't want to cry out, she knew this was hurting Alastair just as much as her. This bitch was using her to cause Alastair pain. But the next cut was deeper, and this time she couldn't help but cry out.

"That's a pretty sound," Diana crooned.

"Stop." Alastair jumped to his feet, his chair toppling

over. He slammed into one of the guards. "Stop hurting her."

Darcy's insides turned hollow. This was his nightmare. Diana was forcing him to relive it. At that moment, Darcy hated Diana Acton with the force of a thousand suns.

As Alastair struggled against his guards, Darcy pressed her hands into her thighs, digging deep to try and find some control.

That's when she felt her back-up mini-tablet in her pocket.

Alastair made a tortured sound and went crazy. He tossed one guard against the wall and rammed into the other one.

Another slice of the knife and Darcy groaned, slipping her fingers surreptitiously into her pocket. She fought back against the wave of agony. Her fingers brushed the tablet.

She couldn't see what she was doing, but she'd memorized her tablet screen. She visualized the buttons. She prayed the guards didn't notice.

"Let her go!" Alastair roared. "Stop."

"Shoot him in the leg," Diana ordered calmly.

The loud report of a gun was deafening in the small space.

"No!" Terrified, Darcy turned her head. She saw Alastair fall to the floor. With his hands cuffed behind his back, he couldn't put pressure on his wound. Blood welled.

The guard who'd shot him moved, aiming his weapon at Alastair's head.

Alastair stared into Darcy's face. "I love you, Darcy."

Her mouth dropped open. *Oh, God.* He loved her. Warmth flooded her. This strong, dedicated, handsome man loved her. He'd always fight to help people in trouble and stop the bad guys, but she knew he had room in his heart for her. She loved the protector in him. She had finally found the love she'd been searching for—not a fairy tale, but something deep and true.

Boy, he'd picked a really bad time to tell her.

"How sweet," Diana sneered.

Darcy glowered at the woman. "You don't know anything about love, or sacrifice, or caring."

"My family is everything to me!"

Darcy shook her head. "You care about nothing but yourself and power. That's selfish. Love is never selfish."

Darcy turned her head and smiled at Alastair. "I think I love you back."

His brows drew together. "You think?"

"I still need a little more convincing. I know you can be very persuasive when it suits you." She looked around the room. "I also need a trip to the beach after this. Somewhere with no bad guys. Somewhere I can get wet." She looked into his face and rolled her eyes to the ceiling. She mentally urged him to understand her words.

"You'll be dead after this." Diana raised the knife again.

"I don't think so." Darcy pressed on her tablet screen. *Please be the right command.*

The overhead fire sprinklers flared to life, dousing the room with water.

The guards shouted and Darcy kicked out. She broke free and swung off the table.

She charged at Diana, slamming into the woman and knocking her over. Darcy snatched up the diamond case and rushed across the room to Alastair.

She saw he was free of his cuffs. How the hell had he done that? He rammed the final guard into the wall, and she heard the man's skull thud on the plaster. His body slid down the wall to the floor.

"Alastair!"

He grabbed her hand. "Come on." He grabbed the overturned chair, dragging it behind them. Once they moved into the hall, he slammed the door closed, and wedged the chair under the door handle.

"How'd you get free of the cuffs?"

"I always carry a spare handcuff key. I like to be prepared." He pulled her shirt closed and tied it. "Are you all right?"

"Yes. Your leg?" There was a lot of blood.

"It'll hold. Now move."

"So bossy." They moved down the hall. Alastair was limping badly. His trouser leg was soaked with blood and worry nipped at her.

"Keep moving," he said.

They came out in a casual living area filled with cream-colored couches. At the far end was a pair of sliding doors that opened onto another deck.

They were sailing down the Potomac. God, the river was huge.

"Let's look for some sort of escape raft or speedboat—"

"Darcy." Alastair collapsed against the back of a couch, smearing blood on the fabric. "I can't go any farther."

"No."

"You need to go. Get to safety."

Her heart lodged in her throat. "No!"

CHAPTER FIFTEEN

"You get up, Burke." Darcy raced over to a cabinet, yanking out drawers.

Alastair watched her, breathing through the pain. She came back with a kitchen towel and wadded it against his leg.

Just making his way down the hall had taken it out of him. His leg was pure torture.

"Get out, Darcy. Find a boat, and go and get help."

She shook her head, her dark hair brushing her jaw. "You know I'm bad with orders. I'm *not* leaving the man I love to die."

His heart filled with electric warmth. Darcy loved him. But terror followed. She wasn't going to leave.

He looked at the blood staining her white shirt. She looked like an extra from a horror movie. If he lost her, he wouldn't survive. Watching that woman torture Darcy while there was nothing he could do... It had almost broken him.

"Hey." Darcy cupped his cheeks. "Stay with me."

He nodded.

"Let's get out of here," she said. "Together. I guess if you can't go any farther, then I'll just have to rescue you."

"You already have."

Her head snapped up, warmth suffusing her face. She leaned forward and kissed him.

"I'm going to spend a lot more time kissing you later. Now, let's go." She looked around, then she rushed over to the sliding doors.

Steeling himself against the pain, Alastair limped over to join her.

But before she could open the doors more than a few inches, the main door to the room burst open.

"Give me my diamonds!" Diana strode across the space, several guards flanking her.

Gunfire sprayed the walls.

Alastair tackled Darcy to the floor, knocking his injured leg in the process. The pain was outrageous and his vision blurred. He breathed through his mouth, praying he wouldn't puke.

Then, the hard muzzle of a gun pressed to the back of his head.

When he looked up, he saw another guard holding a gun to Darcy's temple. Her face was pale.

No. It couldn't end like this.

Diana snatched the case out of Darcy's hands and opened it.

"These are mine."

The lights went out. Daylight from outside was the only source of light. Alastair glanced at Darcy.

She shook her head. "That wasn't me."

Suddenly, a small, silver ball flew in from outside. It hit the floor, then rolled. A high-pitched sound filled the room.

Everyone started screaming. *Fuck*. Alastair gritted his teeth. It was like an ice pick being driven into his ears. He clapped his hands over his ears, trying to block the sound. He saw Darcy doing the same, her face contorted with pain.

Suddenly, the sliding glass doors shattered.

Alastair glanced up. Outside, ropes dropped from the sky and black-clad soldiers rappelled onto the deck. As soon as their boots hit wood, they unclipped and strode into the room.

The newcomers wore black scarves over the bottom half of their faces and carried futuristic-looking assault rifles.

They engaged the Silk Road guards, hard and fast.

Alastair knew instantly who they were. Team 52.

The piercing sound suddenly stopped. Alastair turned his head and recognized the tall form of Lachlan Hunter, the leader of Team 52. He was holding the silver ball in the palm of his hand.

The man's hand was made of silver metal, as well.

"Darcy." Dec stepped into the room, crouching down in front of them. He slung his rifle onto his back. The rest of the THS team appeared as well.

"No one left to shoot?" Morgan said, clearly disappointed.

"These fuckers hogged the action." Logan glared at the Team 52 members.

Darcy was shaking her head to clear it. "Dec, I'm okay. But they shot Alastair. Bullet wound to his thigh."

Alastair groaned as he put his back to the wall. Blood was smeared all over him and the floor. Darcy gripped his arm.

"Kimura," Hunter bit out.

A black-clad man dropped down beside Alastair and he looked up. Not a man, a woman. Gray eyes looked at him over her scarf. She was opening a backpack.

"I'm a medic." She reached out to touch his gunshot wound.

"Her first." He nodded at Darcy.

Darcy's chin lifted. "No." She rose to her knees.

Dec and Cal hissed.

"What the fuck, Darcy!" Dec ground out.

Everyone now had an unobstructed view of her shirt. It was soaked in blood.

"Tell me that isn't yours," Cal said.

"Um, I have a few cuts courtesy of the Collector, but it isn't as bad as it looks."

"Here." The Team 52 medic pressed a wad of gauze to her belly. "Keep the pressure on." Then the woman turned back to Alastair's leg. She tore his trouser leg open.

Darcy nudged her brothers back and leaned against Alastair's side. She reached up and kissed him. "I love you."

Cal groaned. "Shit."

Dec groaned as well.

From nearby, Alastair noticed Morgan and Logan

grinning. Ronin and Hale were shaking their heads, looking amused.

"Hunter," Alastair called out.

The Team 52 leader inclined his head.

"How the hell did you get here?"

"I thought you might need some help."

"The Collector," Alastair said. "It's Diana Acton, Henry Acton's daughter."

Darcy scanned the room, her eyes widening. "Where did she go?"

"She can't have gone far," Dec said. "The yacht is surrounded by FBI and—" he glanced at Team 52 "—others."

"She has a collection," Alastair continued. "Artifacts you need to know about."

Hunter's scary-flat gold eyes flashed. "We'll take care of it."

Dec picked up the diamond case and opened it. "Fuck."

The Black Orlov was missing.

Alastair looked at the medic. "You got any drugs in there to get me on my feet?"

The woman tilted her head. "Maybe."

"Give some to me and someone help me up," Alastair barked.

"He has a hard time with his manners," Darcy said.

"We have to find Acton," Alastair said. "Now!"

DARCY WATCHED her brothers helping Alastair hobble along the corridor.

Beside them, the Team 52 leader, Hunter, touched his ear. "She's on the roof."

Their small group continued onward and moved up the stairs leading to the top deck. Darcy bit her lip, seeing the pain in Alastair's face with each step he took. She glanced at Hunter, and he looked back at her with golden eyes that nearly made her shiver. Like a tiger's eyes...just before he attacked you.

They pushed through a door and out into the sunshine.

As they spilled out onto the top deck, she spotted Diana Acton. The woman was up on the roof of the bridge, clinging to an antenna.

What the hell?

The Black Orlov necklace was around her neck.

"What is she doing?" Darcy asked.

"She's lost it," Dec muttered.

"You can't stop me!" Diana called out. "Silk Road will be the most powerful group in the world."

Alastair pushed away from Dec and Cal, and limped forward. He stood tall beside Hunter.

"It's over, Diana."

"Never!"

"We have your son in custody."

"My lawyers will have him free in just a few hours."

Hunter shifted. "Actually, he's been taken into custody by my team. We plan to interrogate him about the contents and location of your collection."

The woman shook her head. "He'll never talk."

"We have our ways." Hunter cocked his head. "We're a black ops team, Ms. Acton. Off the books, with our own set of rules. No lawyer will ever find him."

The woman clutched at the necklace. "I have the Black Orlov. I'll use it to defeat you all."

"It's a diamond. It has no powers." Alastair stared at the woman. "It's time to give up."

"I won't," the woman whispered. "My father never did."

"You've hurt too many people." Alastair's tone was hard. "You've destroyed too many families, and stolen pieces of history that belong to everyone in this world. It ends today."

"No."

"You left other children with no fathers, no mothers. You did the very thing you were trying to avenge."

A look crossed the woman's face and she shook her head.

Darcy saw Alastair waver on his leg. She moved to him and pressed in close to his side. He wrapped an arm around her shoulders, looked down at her and put a little bit of his weight on her. She smiled.

"No more mothers will die," Darcy said. "After today, Silk Road won't hurt anyone else."

Alastair nodded. "Everyone on this deck will work tirelessly to dismantle Silk Road, piece by piece. Until there's nothing left. Until it's just an ugly, forgotten footnote in a dusty file. And you'll be wasting away in a prison cell for the rest of your life."

"No." Now the woman sounded horrified, her face pale.

She pushed away from the antenna and moved shakily toward the edge of the roof.

"Shit," Alastair muttered.

Darcy could see the woman's face had gone slack, her eyes staring off into the distance.

The men on the deck started moving, but before they even had a chance to get close, Diana jumped.

She didn't make it to the water. And to Darcy, it looked like she wasn't even aiming for it.

Darcy turned away, the thump of Diana's body hitting the deck a horrifying sound.

Alastair pulled Darcy close, pressed her face against his chest.

"Oh, God."

"Don't look." He ran a hand up her back.

A moment later, Hunter and his medic appeared.

"She's dead." Hunter held the Black Orlov in his gloved hand.

"You giving that back to me?" Alastair asked.

"No. I think it's safer if I hold on to it."

Darcy looked up and gasped. "It really is ancient technology?"

Hunter's eyes crinkled and she guessed the man was smiling. What he didn't do was answer her question. "And don't think I've forgotten about the tracker you placed on the diamond."

Darcy wrinkled her nose. "I assume you know how to remove it."

"I think we can figure it out." Then he turned, calling for his team.

"Well, he's Mr. Mysterious, isn't he?" she muttered.

"That's his job."

"He scares me."

Alastair nodded. "He scares me, too."

As Team 52 moved away, Darcy let out a shaky breath. "It's over."

Alastair tipped her face up to his. "Silk Road is over." He glanced along the length of the ship. "I think my mom would be happy."

Darcy gripped his shoulders. "She would be. And she'd be proud of you. I am."

He pressed his forehead to hers. "I couldn't have done it without you. I think she'd mostly be happy as hell that I found a woman as amazing as you."

Darcy shot him a sassy smile. "Well, of course."

Alastair barked out a laugh and her smile widened. It was starting to sound a little less rusty.

"Want to get out of here?" he asked.

She tightened her hold on him. "Well, since you asked so nicely..."

CHAPTER SIXTEEN

As they walked into the Dashwood, the director hurried over.

"Oh, thank the Lord." The harried-looking man took the diamond case from Alastair and opened it.

He gasped at the empty space and looked up. "The Black Orlov?"

"You'll be contacted about it, Mr. Monroe," Alastair told the man. "It's in safe hands, and the museum will be compensated."

The director pursed his lips, but he nodded.

Alastair tightened his arm around Darcy. They'd both had a trip to the hospital, courtesy of her brothers. His leg wound, and Darcy's cuts, had been treated and bandaged. But they hadn't had a chance to change and they still looked like hell.

"Darcy," a voice called out.

In seconds, they were surrounded by people. He watched as Darcy was engulfed by her parents, sisters-in-law, and friends. Dec and the rest of the THS gang watched and smiled.

"We're fine." Darcy stepped back to Alastair's side. "And the best thing of all, Silk Road is done."

Cheers went up.

"It's true?" Elin appeared beside Alastair. "They're done?"

He nodded. The group had killed Elin's father, and destroyed her mother's art restoration career. Elin had been searching for justice, just like Alastair.

"Really. The Collector was a woman named Diana Acton. She's dead."

"Suicide," Darcy said.

Elin gasped.

"She was wearing the Black Orlov," Darcy added.

Layne leaned forward. "Do you think—?"

Darcy shrugged and lowered her voice. "Team 52 confiscated the necklace."

From behind Elin, Hale scowled. "I do *not* like those guys."

Elin patted his chest. "So they screwed up in Africa. You have to let it go, Hale."

"I hate them too," Logan said.

Morgan rolled her eyes. "You hate everything."

"He doesn't hate me." Sydney was grinning, and Logan pulled her up on her toes for a wet kiss.

Click.

Alastair turned his head at the sound. Dani Ward was taking photos.

"To mark the occasion," the photographer said. "The end of Silk Road."

"Drinks tonight," Morgan called out.

From beside Morgan, Zach shook his head, a smile on his handsome face. "Pretty sure there'll be some hangovers on the flight home tomorrow."

Darcy smiled. "I can't believe it. Silk Road is gone."

Alastair tightened his arm around her. "Believe it."

Their gazes met and he felt need stir. He'd come close to losing her today, and he'd learned just how much she meant to him.

Love. The one thing he'd guarded himself against, and Darcy Ward had plowed through all his well-built walls. He really wanted to drag her back to his place and have her all to himself.

He pulled her up on her toes, and she eagerly met his mouth with her own.

Alastair tried to keep the kiss respectable, but her hands slid into his hair, and she kissed him back eagerly.

All around, cheers and whistles broke out.

He pulled back. Everyone was grinning at them... Except for Dec and Cal, who both looked pained.

Logan scowled. "I thought you hated him, Darcy?"

Darcy smoothed a hand over Alastair's shoulder. "I changed my mind. I love him."

More cheers.

"About time," Sydney said.

Layne bumped a hip against Dani. "You owe me fifty bucks."

Alastair pressed his lips to Darcy's ear. "I love you too, baby."

"So..." Her face changed, and for the first time since he'd known Darcy Ward, she looked nervous.

His gut tightened. "What?"

She fiddled with a button on his shirt. "Well, you live and work in DC, and I live and work in Denver..."

Alastair had already thought that problem through. Seeing the woman he loved being tortured in front of him sure put things in perspective.

"I hear that the FBI has an office in Denver."

She stilled. "You'd move? For me?"

"For us." He kissed her again. "But yes, I'd do anything for you. Even hack your system, bribe you into working for me so I could see you every day, and drive you crazy."

Her eyes widened. "You are so arrogant and annoying—"

He covered her mouth with his, and this time, he didn't hear the cheers. There was only Darcy.

DARCY ROLLED OVER IN BED, golden Denver sunshine shining through the blinds she'd forgotten to close the night before.

Warm skin pressed against her back and a hand slid into her panties, stroking between her legs.

She moaned, trying to roll to face Alastair. But he held her in place, her back pressed to his front.

"Be careful of your leg," she said.

He kissed her neck, his diabolical fingers still caressing her. "Yes, ma'am."

A month had passed since the final showdown with Diana Acton and Silk Road. The wound on his thigh was much better, but still healing. Her cuts had scabbed over and healed. She'd have scars, but Darcy was too happy to care.

Alastair had worked hard for several weeks to wrap up the Silk Road case. The FBI, with some behind-the-scenes help—she suspected from Team 52, but Alastair hadn't said—had dismantled the last of the syndicate's operations. William Acton was locked away and not getting out for a very long time.

Diana Acton's private collection had been found. Certain items had been locked away, others returned to their rightful owners, and the rest donated to certain museums. The Dashwood Museum had received some choice pieces in lieu of the Black Orlov.

Alastair had transferred to the FBI office in Denver and was still working for the Art Crime Team. He was also enjoying the opportunity to work with Elin again.

His fingers stroked higher and Darcy moaned. He found her clit and sensations rocketed through her. Her thoughts scattered.

This time, she pushed harder and rolled to face him. She nudged him onto his back and climbed on top.

"You're still recovering." She straddled his thighs. "I'll have to do all the work."

His gaze was at half mast, a smile on his lips. He was smiling a lot more these days. "If you expect me to complain, you're wrong."

She gripped her shirt—his T-shirt—and yanked it over her head. Then she quickly rose and shimmied out of her panties.

He lay there, stretched out on the bed watching her.

The unabashed appreciation in his eyes turned her on. She let her gaze slide down that sexy body of his. She reached out and scratched her nails over his hard abs.

All hers.

She lifted her hips and sank down on his thick cock. She moaned. She loved being filled up by him.

"I've never seen anything sexier—" his voice was a deep drawl "—than you taking me inside your hot little body."

Darcy leaned forward, pressing her palms to his chest, and started riding him. They'd both had health checks and had ditched the condoms. She loved having nothing between them. "Alastair—"

"Faster, Darcy." His hands clamped on her hips.

"So bossy."

"You love it."

"So arrogant."

His hand moved lower and found her clit. She bit back a cry, moving faster.

"Hold on, Darcy," he ordered. "Don't come yet."

Emotions churned inside her. "I...can't." Her release was rushing closer. That sweet, addictive promise of pleasure.

"I want us to come together," he said. "Hold it."

She moaned, her gaze locking with his.

He was hers. The man she'd grow old with. The man who'd love her forever. The man who loved her passionately, completely.

A man she respected, and for all his annoying arrogance, loved and respected her.

She was so close to coming. "Alastair—"

"Come. Come now, baby."

She threw her head back and cried out.

As Darcy rode through her pleasure, she heard his long, answering groan as he came. She collapsed against him, careful not to jostle his thigh. He stroked his hands down her back.

"Damn, I'm so glad I hacked your system, Darcy Ward."

She laughed. "Is that what they're calling it these days?"

His arms tightened on her. "Love you."

"Love you right back, my Agent Arrogant and Slightly-less-annoying."

His full-bodied laughter made her smile.

ALASTAIR LOOKED at Lachlan Hunter's face on his computer screen.

"The last of Silk Road's artifacts have been secured," Hunter said, over the secure line.

"Good. Thanks for your help with this. How's the rest of your team?" Alastair had seen the strange news reports out of LA and suspected Team 52 had been sent in to clean up.

A faint smile touched the man's lips. "Busy. And I have a man on leave. On his honeymoon."

Alastair smiled. "I know how that goes."

Hunter nodded, a warm look moving through his golden eyes. "Me, too."

"If you ever need my help, you've got it," Alastair said.

"Same, Burke. Any time."

The screen went black, and Alastair sat back in his chair. He looked at the stack of files on his desk. He planned to power through his work and get home early to cook his woman an extra-special dinner.

There was a knock on his door and Elin poked her head in.

"Hey, how's the new office?"

"Fine."

The woman smiled. "Glad you're here, Alastair. Although Thom is missing you. He keeps sending me sad emails."

"He got a promotion, so he's too busy to miss me." Alastair had no doubt he'd work with Thom again someday.

"And I'm glad you and Darcy finally finished your wild mating dance." Elin winked and left.

Alastair shook his head. He had a job he loved, good friends, and a new family. He hadn't been too sure about inheriting two brothers, but he, Dec, and Cal were working things out. The men liked to offer pointers on dealing with a riled Darcy. He smiled. They also loved to share stories about when she was younger.

But best of all, Alastair had a woman he loved.

His gaze moved to the framed picture of him and his mom that was now sitting on his desk. Beside it, was one of him and Darcy. He was sitting in a chair and she was leaning over him from behind, her chin resting on his shoulder. There was a beaming smile on her face.

"I'm good, Mom. I'm sorry you never got to meet her, but she's perfect."

"Who's perfect?"

Darcy's voice startled him, but he managed to control his reaction. He looked at his monitor and saw her face on the screen.

"Darcy?"

"Hello there, handsome."

"Please tell me you didn't hack the FBI's computer system."

"Who me?" She batted her eyelids.

He wasn't buying that innocent look at all.

"I just wanted to see my special agent and say hello."

She was so beautiful, and he was such a lucky bastard. "Hi."

"I wanted to see if you had time for lunch today?" she asked.

He glanced at his calendar. "Yeah. I can pick you up at the THS office."

She smiled. "Perfect." She lowered her voice. "And I'll need you to bring something special for me."

That sultry tone made his gut tighten. "Anything."

"Can you please bring me a vanilla latte? Extra shot." She winked and the screen blinked off.

And Alastair just sat there grinning.

An hour later, he parked in front of the converted warehouse that housed the THS offices. He grabbed the two trays of coffee he'd picked up from Darcy's favorite coffee shop, and headed for the front door.

"Afternoon."

Oliver Ward was standing on the front steps.

"Professor." Alastair tried not to feel awkward. But he was sleeping with the man's daughter.

"Please, Oliver is fine."

"Cappuccino?" Alastair held out one of the trays. "I bought extra."

Oliver took one. "Clearly, you know my daughter well."

Together, they walked inside, and the sound of raised voices hit them. Darcy and Dec were arguing.

"It's a decent, paying job, Declan."

"It's boring work, Darce. Babysitting some rich woman's jewelry?" Dec made a gagging sound.

"I'm sorry it's not exciting enough for you former Navy SEAL badasses, but we have bills to pay."

Alastair stepped into the fray. "Coffee?"

"Babe." Darcy hustled over, heels clicking on the floor.

He held up a latte, but pulled it back as she reached for it. "Kiss first."

She threw her arms around his neck and planted her lips on his. She took her time, kissing him thoroughly.

"God." Dec was looking at the ceiling.

"Suck it up, bro," Darcy said. "On our girls' nights out, I have to listen to your wife praise your stamina."

Layne's cheeks turned pink.

Looking pleased with herself, Darcy turned back to Alastair. "How was your morning, Special Agent Burke?"

"Brilliant."

Her face softened. "Happy?"

"Yeah."

"Can I have my latte now?"

His gaze swiveled to the cup and suddenly he was hit with nerves. "Well..."

The front door opened. Distracted, Darcy looked past him and smiled at the man who'd entered.

"Hi, welcome to Treasure Hunter Security, I'm Darcy."

"Darcy Ward?" The man, who looked about forty with thinning hair and an expensive suit, stood in the lobby, out of the line of sight of the rest of the THS crew. His gaze skated over Alastair and sharpened on Darcy.

Instantly, Alastair didn't like the man.

She stepped forward. "Yes."

The man held up a gun and aimed it at her.

Alastair stiffened. He took a step back and signaled to Dec, who went on alert. The rest of the THS team tensed, pulling their weapons.

"My name is Donald Simmons." The man's tone was hard and firm. "I'm taking over from Silk Road, and I need some information."

Darcy cocked a hip. "Really?"

No fear. That was his Darcy. "Darcy—" Alastair warned.

She held her palm up in his direction and kept staring at Simmons. "So, you think now that Silk Road is gone, you're going to fill the void? Make some money off being an asshole and stealing antiquities?"

The man's bushy brows drew together. "Yeah. I want all the information you have on any treasures. The valuable ones."

"No."

"No?" The man's face started turning red.

"I want to drink my latte and have lunch with my man." She pointed at Alastair. "My hot, FBI Special Agent boyfriend."

Simmons' eyes widened and flicked to Alastair.

Alastair felt several presences move in behind him.

Darcy shifted, her hair swinging. "And behind him are my two brothers. Former Navy SEALs."

Simmons' face paled.

More movement. "And behind them, are my friends and employees. Also former Navy SEALs. Except Morgan, she's just a badass."

Morgan smiled and tossed the man a two-fingered salute.

Simmons looked green now, and his gun wavered in his hand.

Darcy moved fast and smacked the gun out of the man's fingers. Dec and Cal charged forward, quickly subduing the man.

Darcy swiveled and smiled at Alastair. "Coffee, now."

He handed it to her.

With Darcy in his life, he knew there would always be some drama or adventure going on. He couldn't wait for more.

She rattled the cup. "It's empty." She frowned. "There's something in here."

"Open it," he said.

Raising a brow, she pulled off the lid. Then her mouth fell open. She reached in and pulled out the diamond ring. It was a simple, elegant design—a platinum band with a single, large princess-cut stone.

Her gaze met his. "Alastair."

"Be mine, Darcy Ward." He grabbed her hand. "Make a life with me. Forever."

He took the ring from her slightly trembling fingers and lifted her left hand.

Her eyes glimmered. "Yes, my Agent Arrogant and Annoying. I'll marry you."

Happiness welling in his chest, Alastair slipped the ring on her finger. Then he swept her close, dipped her back, and kissed her.

All around, their family and friends clapped and cheered. Except for Dec and Cal.

"Shit," Dec muttered.

"Crap," Cal grumbled.

But both brothers were smiling.

EPILOGUE

Darcy sipped her champagne as Logan complained about his tuxedo. Again.

"Enough, Mr. Grumpy," Sydney slapped his arm. "Hold your daughter." She handed the baby over.

Logan expertly tucked his four-month-old, sleeping daughter into the crook of his brawny arm.

God, the look on his face. Darcy had never expected to see the rough, tough Logan O'Connor look more besotted than when he looked at his wife. But any time the man was near his daughter, Hanna, the big man melted.

"How's the gorgeous bride?" Dani leaned over and clicked her glass against Darcy's. Dani's was filled with sparkling juice since she was sporting a baby bump under her blue dress.

"I'm awesome." Darcy ran a hand down her sleek, strapless Vera Wang gown.

"And gorgeous," Dani said.

"Thank you. Where's your camera?"

Dani's nose wrinkled. "My husband confiscated it."

They both looked across the ballroom at Cal. He was standing with Dec—both her brothers looking ridiculously handsome in their tuxedos. As did her husband.

Her husband. Darcy stared at Alastair. God, she never got tired of looking at the man. He was still rugged and serious, but he smiled a lot more now.

He was deep in intense conversation with her brothers.

"Looks like your brothers are trying to convince your man to quit the FBI and join THS," Dani said. "Again."

Darcy smiled. To everyone's amusement and no one's surprise, over the last year and a half, her brothers and Alastair had bonded, and become good friends.

"My feet are killing me," a female voice said.

Darcy looked up. Sloan looked gorgeous in her blue-gray bridesmaid's gown. A stunning emerald engagement ring rested on her finger.

"But you look fantastic. Have another drink." Darcy shoved another glass of champagne at her friend.

Zach and Morgan whizzed past on the dance floor. As Darcy watched, the laughing couple bumped into Hale and Elin, who were also dancing. Hale and Elin were in the midst of planning their wedding. Morgan had announced that she was fine with having hot sex with her hot, sexy professor, and wasn't planning to ruin a good thing by getting hitched.

Darcy's parents danced past next, moving in perfect sync. Her heart filled to bursting. She understood their love even better now that she had Alastair. One day, she knew she'd spin around in her husband's strong arms as they danced at their children's weddings. She hoped Alastair still looked at her the way her dad looked at her mom.

Ronin and Peri appeared. Peri's copper-colored hair was mussed.

"Hey," the woman said.

Darcy tried to hide her laughter.

"Oh, my God." Dani shook her head and grinned. "Please don't tell me you guys just had hot wedding-reception sex."

Ronin's expression didn't change. The man had the best poker face Darcy had ever seen.

Peri's cheeks filled with color and her lips quirked. "Maybe."

Suddenly, across the dance floor, Darcy saw a harried-looking Layne running through the crowd. "Emmy, no!"

Darcy looked down and spotted her baby niece, wearing a pink, frilly dress, crawling at top speed onto the dance floor.

Darcy gasped. There was no way the dancers would spot the eight-month-old down on the floor. She was in danger of being trampled.

Fatherly instinct kicking in, Dec stiffened and lifted his head. He spotted his precious baby girl, but he was too far away to get to her.

Darcy was already moving, but she knew she'd never make it before someone ran over the tiny girl.

Alastair was closest to the dance floor. He dived, slid along the floor, and scooped the little girl into his arms. A few startled dancers stumbled out of the way. Alastair and Emmy slid another few feet before they came to a stop.

Emmy shot her new uncle a gummy grin, showing off two tiny baby teeth, and clapped her hands with glee.

"Careful, Princess." Alastair grinned back and ran a hand over her silky hair.

Darcy smiled. Her husband was besotted by Layne and Dec's offspring. It was far too easy to imagine him cradling his own daughter. *One day.*

He rose to his feet and handed the girl off to her daddy. Then Alastair's green eyes locked with Darcy's.

Heedless of the other dancers, he strode toward her. "Hello, Mrs. Burke."

She shivered. She *loved* hearing that. "Hello, Special Agent Burke. Saving little ladies in distress at every turn, hm?"

"All part of the job, ma'am." He winked at her. "Would you like to dance?"

"Yes." She took her husband's hand. The man who challenged, supported, and loved her every second of every day.

The man who looked at her with love in his eyes, like she was the most precious treasure he'd ever seen.

Then he wrapped his arms around her, and they moved across the dance floor in perfect sync. And Darcy knew she never wanted to be anywhere else.

I hope you enjoyed Darcy and Alastair's story!

Thank you so much for joining me on all the *Treasure Hunter Security* adventures. I loved writing this series and combining so many of the things I love: action, adventure, history, travel, tough heroes, smart heroines, and of course, happily ever afters.

We might be finished with *Treasure Hunter Security* but there are more adventures to come — including those of the Team 52 gang! And expect a few cameos from Dec, Darcy, Alastair, and the THS guys.

For more action-packed adventure, read on for a preview of ***Mission: Her Protection*** (Team 52 #1) to check out Lachlan Hunter's wild ride.

Don't miss out! For updates about new releases, action romance info, free books, and other fun stuff, sign up for my VIP mailing list and get your *free box set* containing three action-packed romances.

Visit here to get started: www.annahackettbooks.com

PREVIEW - MISSION: HER PROTECTION

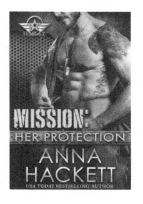

It was a beautiful day—ten below zero, and ice as far as the eye could see.

Dr. Rowan Schafer tugged at the fur-lined hood of her arctic parka, and stared across the unforgiving landscape of Ellesmere Island, the northernmost island in Canada. The Arctic Circle lay about fifteen hundred miles to the south, and large portions of the island were covered with glaciers and ice.

Rowan breathed in the fresh, frigid air. There was nowhere else she wanted to be.

Hefting her small pickaxe, she stepped closer to the wall of glacial ice in front of her. The retreating Gilman Glacier was proving a fascinating location. Her multi-disciplinary team of hydrologists, glaciologists, geophysicists, botanists, and climate scientists were more than happy to brave the cold for the chance to carry out their varied research projects. She began to chip away at the ice once more, searching for any interesting samples.

"Rowan."

She spun and saw one of the members of her team headed her way. Dr. Isabel Silva's parka was red like the rest of the team's, but she wore a woolen hat in a shocking shade of pink over her black hair. Originally from Brazil, Rowan knew the paleobotanist disliked the cold.

"What's the latest, Isabel?" Rowan asked.

"The sled on the snowmobile is almost full of samples." The woman waved her hand in the air, like she always did when she was talking. "You should have seen the moss and lichen samples I pulled. There were loads of them in area 3-41. I can't *wait* to get started on the tests." She shivered. "And be out of this blasted cold."

Rowan suppressed a smile. *Scientists*. She had her own degrees in hydrology and biology, with a minor in paleontology that had shocked her very academic parents. But on this expedition, she was here as leader to keep her team of fourteen fed, clothed, and alive.

"Okay, well, you and Dr. Fournier can run the samples back to base, and then come back to collect me and Dr. Jensen."

Isabel broke into a smile. "You know Lars has a crush on you."

Dr. Lars Jensen was a brilliant, young geophysicist. And yes, Rowan hadn't missed his not-so-subtle attempts to ask her out.

"I'm not here looking for dates."

"But he's kind of cute." Isabel grinned and winked. "In a nerdy kind of way."

Rowan's mouth firmed. Lars was also several years younger than her and, while sweet, didn't interest her in that way. Besides, she'd had enough of people trying to set her up. Her mother was always trying to push various *appropriate* men on Rowan—men with the right credentials, the right degrees, and the right tenured positions. Neither of her parents cared about love or passion; they just cared about how many dissertations and doctorates people collected. Their daughter included.

She dragged in a breath. That was why she'd applied for this expedition—for a chance to get away, a chance for some adventure. "Finish with the samples, Isabel, then—"

Shouts from farther down the glacier had both women spinning. The two other scientists, their red coats bright against the white ice, were waving their arms.

"Wonder what they've found?" Rowan started down the ice.

Isabel followed. "Probably the remains of a mammoth or a mastodon. The weirdest things turn these guys on."

Careful not to move too fast on the slippery surface, Rowan and Isabel reached the men.

"Dr. Schafer, you have to see this." Lars' blue eyes were bright, his nose red from the cold.

She crouched beside Dr. Marc Fournier. "What have you got?"

The older hydrologist scratched carefully at the ice with his pickaxe. "I have no idea." His voice lilted with his French accent.

Rowan studied the discovery. Suspended in the ice, the circular object was about the size of her palm. It was dull-gray in color, and just the edge of it was protruding through the ice, thanks to the warming temperatures that were causing the glacier to retreat.

She touched the end of it with her gloved hand. It was firm, but smooth. "It's not wood, or plant life."

"Maybe stone?" Marc tapped it gently with the axe and it made a metallic echo.

Rowan blinked. "It can't be metal."

"The ice here is about five thousand years old," Lars breathed.

Rowan stood. "Let's get it out."

With her arms crossed, she watched the scientists carefully work the ice away from the object. She knew that several thousand years ago, the fjords of the Hazen Plateau were populated by the mysterious and not-well understood Pre-Dorset and Dorset cultures. They'd made their homes in the Arctic, hunted and used simple tools. The Dorset disappeared when the Thule—ancestors to the Inuit—arrived, much later. Even the Viking Norse had once had communities on Ellesmere and neighboring Greenland.

Most of those former settlements had been near the coast. Scanning the ice around them, she thought it unlikely that there would have been settlements up here.

And certainly not settlements that worked metal. The early people who'd made their home on Ellesmere hunted sea mammals like seals or land mammals like caribou.

Still, she was a scientist, and she knew better than to make assumptions without first gathering all the facts. Her drill team, who were farther up on the ice, were extracting ice core samples. Their studies were showing that roughly five thousand years ago, temperatures here were warmer than they were today. That meant the ice and glaciers on the island would have retreated then as well, and perhaps people had made their homes farther north than previously thought.

Marc pulled the object free with careful movements. It was still coated in a thin layer of ice.

"Are those markings?" Isabel breathed.

They sure looked like it. Rowan studied the scratches carved into the surface of the object. They looked like they could be some sort of writing or glyphs, but if that was the case, they were like nothing she'd ever seen before.

Lars frowned. "I don't know. They could just be natural scoring, or erosion grooves."

Rowan pushed a few errant strands of her dark-red hair off her face. "Since none of us are archeologists, we're going to need an expert to take a look at it."

"It's probably five thousand years old," Isabel added. "If it is man-made, with writing on it, it'll blow all accepted historical theories out of the water."

"Let's not get ahead of ourselves," Rowan said calmly. "It needs to be examined first. It could be natural."

"Or alien," Lars added.

As one, they swiveled to look at the younger man.

He shrugged, his cheeks turning red. "Just saying. Odds are that we aren't alone in this universe. If—"

"Enough." Rowan straightened, knowing once Lars got started on a subject, it was hard to get him to stop. "Pack it up, get it back to base, and store it with the rest of the samples. I'll make some calls." It killed her to put it aside, but this mystery object wasn't their top priority. They had frozen plant and seed samples, and ice samples, that they needed to get back to their research labs.

Every curious instinct inside Rowan was singing, wanting to solve the mystery. God, if she had discovered something that threw accepted ancient history theories out, her parents would be horrified. She'd always been interested in archeology, but her parents had almost had heart attacks when she'd told them. They'd quietly organized other opportunities for her, and before she knew it, she'd been studying hydrology and biology. She'd managed to sneak in her paleontology studies where she could.

Dr. Arthur Caswell and Dr. Kathleen Schafer expected nothing but perfection from their sole progeny. Even after their bloodless divorce, they'd still expected Rowan to do exactly as they wanted.

Rowan had long-ago realized that nothing she ever did would please her parents for long. She blew out a breath. It had taken a painful childhood spent trying to win their love and affection—and failing miserably—to realize that. They were just too absorbed in their own work and lives.

Pull up your big-girl panties, Rowan. She'd never been abused and had been given a great education. She had work she enjoyed, interesting colleagues, and a lot to be thankful for.

Rowan watched her team pack the last of their samples onto the sled. She glanced to the southern horizon, peering at the bank of clouds in the distance. Ellesmere didn't get a lot of precipitation, which meant not a lot of snow, but plenty of ice. Still, it looked like bad weather was brewing and she wanted everyone safely back at camp.

"Okay, everyone, enough for today. Let's head back to base for hot chocolate and coffee."

Isabel rolled her eyes. "You and your chocolate."

Rowan made no apologies for her addiction, or the fact that half her bag for the trip here had been filled with her stash of high-quality chocolate—milk, dark, powdered, and her prized couverture chocolate.

"I want a nip of something warmer," Lars said.

No one complained about leaving. Working out on the ice was bitterly cold, even in September, with the last blush of summer behind them.

Rowan climbed on a snowmobile and quickly grabbed her hand-held radio. "Hazen Team Two, this is Hazen Team One. We are headed back to Hazen Base, confirm."

A few seconds later, the radio crackled. "Acknowledged, Hazen One. We see the clouds, Rowan. We're leaving the drill site now."

Dr. Samuel Malu was as steady and dependable as the sunrise.

"See you there," she answered.

Marc climbed onto the second snowmobile, Lars riding behind him. Rowan waited for Isabel to climb on before firing up the engine. They both pulled their goggles on.

It wasn't a long trip back to base, and soon the camp appeared ahead. Seven large, temporary, polar domes made of high-tech, insulated materials were linked together by short, covered tunnels to make the multi-structure dome camp. The domes housed their living quarters, kitchen and rec room, labs, and one that held Rowan's office, the communications room, and storage. The high-tech insulation made the domes easy to heat, and they were relatively easy to construct and move. The structures had been erected to last through the seven-month expedition.

The two snowmobiles roared close to the largest dome and pulled to a stop.

"Okay, all the samples and specimens to the labs," Rowan directed, holding open the door that led inside. She watched as Lars carefully picked up a tray and headed inside. Isabel and Marc followed with more trays.

Rowan stepped inside and savored the heat that hit her. The small kitchen was on the far side of the rec room, and the center of the dome was crowded with tables, chairs, and sofas.

She unzipped and shrugged off her coat and hung it beside the other red jackets lined up by the door. Next, she stepped out of her big boots and slipped into the canvas shoes she wore inside.

A sudden commotion from the adjoining tunnel had Rowan frowning. *What now?*

A young woman burst from the tunnel. She was dressed in normal clothes, her blonde hair pulled up in a tight ponytail. Emily Wood, their intern, was a student from the University of British Columbia in Vancouver. She got to do all the not-so-glamorous jobs, like logging and labelling the samples, which meant the scientists could focus on their research.

"Rowan, you have to come now!"

"Emily? What's wrong?" Concerned, Rowan gripped the woman's shoulder. She was practically vibrating. "Are you hurt?"

Emily shook her head. "You have to come to Lab Dome 1." She grabbed Rowan's hand and dragged her into the tunnel. "It's *unbelievable*."

Rowan followed. "Tell me what—"

"No. You need to see it with your own eyes."

Seconds later, they stepped into the lab dome. The temperature was pleasant and Rowan was already feeling hot. She needed to strip off her sweater before she started sweating. She spotted Isabel, and another botanist, Dr. Amara Taylor, staring at the main workbench.

"Okay, what's the big issue?" Rowan stepped forward.

Emily tugged her closer. "Look!" She waved a hand with a flourish.

A number of various petri dishes and sample holders sat on the workbench. Emily had been cataloguing all the seeds and frozen plant life they'd pulled out of the glacier.

"These are some of the samples we collected on our first day here." She pointed at the end of the workbench. "Some I completely thawed and had stored for Dr. Taylor to start analyzing."

Amara lifted her dark eyes to Rowan. The botanist was a little older than Rowan, with dark-brown skin, and long, dark hair swept up in a bun. "These plants are five thousand years old."

Rowan frowned and leaned forward. Then she gasped. "Oh my God."

The plants were sprouting new, green shoots.

"They've come back to life." Emily's voice was breathless.

THE CLINK of silverware and excited conversations filled the rec dome. Rowan stabbed at a clump of meat in her stew, eyeing it with a grimace. She loved food, but hated the stuff that accompanied them on expeditions. She grabbed her mug—sweet, rich hot chocolate. She'd made it from her stash with the perfect amount of cocoa. The best hot chocolate needed no less than sixty percent cocoa but no more than eighty.

Across from her, Lars and Isabel weren't even looking at their food or drink.

"Five thousand years old!" Isabel shook her head, her dark hair falling past her shoulders. "Those plants are millennia old, and they've come back to life."

"Amazing," Lars said. "A few years back, a team working south of here on the Teardrop Glacier at Sverdrup Pass brought moss back to life...but it was only four hundred years old."

Isabel and Lars high-fived each other.

Rowan ate some more of her stew. "Russian scientists regenerated seeds found in a squirrel burrow in the Siberian permafrost."

"Pfft," Lars said. "Ours is still cooler."

"They got the plant to flower and it was fertile," Rowan continued, mildly. "The seeds were thirty-two thousand years old."

Isabel pulled a face and Lars looked disappointed.

"And I think they are working on reviving forty-thousand-year-old nematode worms now."

Her team members both pouted.

Rowan smiled and shook her head. "But five-thousand-year-old plant life is nothing to sneeze at, and the Russian flowers required a lot of human intervention to coax them back to life."

Lars perked up. "All we did was thaw and water ours."

Rowan kept eating, listening to the flow of conversation. The others were wondering what other ancient plant life they might find in the glacial ice.

"What if we find a frozen mammoth?" Lars suggested.

"No, a frozen glacier man," Isabel said.

"Like the Ötzi man," Rowan said. "He was over five thousand years old, and found in the Alps. On the border between Italy and Austria."

Amara arrived, setting her tray down. "Glaciers are retreating all over the planet. I had a colleague who uncovered several Roman artifacts from a glacier in the Swiss Alps."

Isabel sat back in her chair. "Maybe we'll find the fountain of youth? Maybe something in these plants we're uncovering could defy aging, or cure cancer."

Rowan raised an eyebrow and smothered a smile. She was as excited as the others about the regeneration of the plants. But her mind turned to the now-forgotten mystery object they'd plucked from the ice. She'd taken some photos of it and its markings. She was itching to take a look at them again.

"I'm going to take another look at the metal object we found," Lars said, stuffing some stew in his mouth.

"Going to check for any messages from aliens?" Isabel teased.

Lars screwed up his nose, then he glanced at Rowan. "Want to join me?"

She was so tempted, but she had a bunch of work piled on her desk. Most important being the supply lists for their next supply drop. She'd send her photos off to an archeologist friend at Harvard, and then spend the rest of her evening banging through her To-Do list.

"I can't tonight. Duty calls." She pushed her chair back and lifted her tray. "I'm going to eat dessert in my office and do some work."

"You mean eat that delicious chocolate of yours that you guard like a hawk," Isabel said.

Rowan smiled. "I promise to make something yummy tomorrow."

"Your brownies," Lars said.

"Chocolate-covered pralines," Isabel said, almost on top of Lars.

Rowan shook her head. Her chocolate creations were gaining a reputation. "I'll surprise you. If anyone needs me, you know where to find me."

"Bye, Rowan."

"Catch you later."

She set the tray on the side table and scraped off her plates. They had a roster for cooking and cleaning duty, and thankfully it wasn't her night. She ignored the dried-out looking chocolate chip cookies, anticipating the block of milk chocolate in her desk drawer. Yep, she had a weakness for chocolate in any form. Chocolate was the most important food group.

As she headed through the tunnels to the smaller dome that housed her office, she listened to the wind howling outside. It sounded like the storm had arrived. She sent up a silent thanks that her entire team was safe and sound in the camp. Since she was the expedition leader, she got her own office, rather than having to share space with the other scientists in the labs.

In her cramped office, she flicked on her lamp and sat down behind her desk. She opened the drawer, pulled out her chocolate, smelled it, and snapped off a piece. She put it in her mouth and savored the flavor.

The best chocolate was a sensory experience. From how it looked—no cloudy old chocolate, please—to how it smelled and tasted. Right now, she enjoyed the intense flavors on her tongue and the smooth, velvety feel. Her mother had never let her have chocolate or other "unhealthy" foods growing up. Rowan had been forced to sneak her chocolate. She remembered her childhood friend, the intense boy from next door who'd always snuck her candy bars when she'd been outside hiding from her parents.

Shaking her head, Rowan reached over and plugged in her portable speaker. Soon she had some blood-pumping rock music filling her space. She smiled, nodding her head to the beat. Her love of rock-and-roll was another thing she'd kept well-hidden from her parents as a teenager. Her mother loved Bach, and her father preferred silence. Rowan had hidden all her albums growing up, and snuck out to concerts while pretending to be on study dates.

Opening her laptop, she scanned her email. Her stomach clenched. Nothing from her parents. She shook her head. Her mother had emailed once...to ask again when Rowan would be finished with her ill-advised jaunt to the Arctic. Her father hadn't even bothered to check she'd arrived safely.

Old news, Rowan. Shaking off old heartache, she uploaded the photos she'd taken to her computer. She took a second to study the photos of her mystery object again.

"What are you?" she murmured.

The carvings on the object could be natural scratches. She zoomed in. It really looked like some sort of writing to her, but if the object was over five thousand years old, then it wasn't likely. She knew the Pre-Dorset and Dorset peoples had been known to carve soapstone and driftwood, but this artifact would have been at the early point of Pre-Dorset history. Hell, it predated cuneiform—the earliest form of writing—which was barely getting going in Sumer when this thing had ended up in the ice.

She searched on her computer and pulled up some images of Sumerian cuneiform. She set the images side by side and studied them, tapped a finger idly against her lip. Some similarities...maybe. She flicked to the next image, chin in hand. She wanted to run a few tests on the object, see exactly what it was made of.

Not your project, Rowan. Instead, she attached the pictures to an email to send to her archeologist friend.

God, she hoped her parents never discovered she was here, pondering ancient markings on an unidentified object. They'd be horrified. Rowan pinched the bridge of her nose. She was a grown woman of thirty-two. Why did she still feel this driving need for her parents' approval?

With a sigh, she rubbed a fist over her chest, then clicked send on the email. Wishing her family was normal was a lost cause. She'd learned that long ago, hiding out in her treehouse with the boy from next door— who'd had a bad homelife as well.

She sank back in her chair and eyed the pile of paper-work on her desk. *Right, work to do.* This was the reason she was in the middle of the Arctic.

Rowan lost herself in her tasks. She took notes, updated inventory sheets, and approved requests.

A vague, unsettling noise echoed through the tunnel. Her music was still pumping, and she lifted her head and frowned, straining to hear.

She turned off her music and stiffened. Were those screams?

She bolted upright. The screams got louder, interspersed with the crash of furniture and breaking glass.

Team 52

Mission: Her Protection
Mission: Her Rescue (coming soon)
Mission: Her Security (coming soon)

READY FOR ANOTHER?

IN THE AFTERMATH OF AN ALIEN INVASION:

HEROES WILL RISE... WHEN THEY HAVE SOMEONE TO LIVE FOR

In the aftermath of a deadly alien invasion, a band of survivors fights on...

In a world gone to hell, Elle Milton—once the darling of the Sydney social scene—has carved a role for herself as the communications officer for the toughest commando team fighting for humanity's survival—Hell Squad. It's her chance to make a difference and make up for horrible past mistakes...despite the fact that its battle-hardened commander never wanted her on his team.

When Hell Squad is tasked with destroying a strategic alien facility, Elle knows they need her skills in the field. But first she must go head to head with Marcus Steele and convince him she won't be a liability.

Marcus Steele is a warrior through and through. He fights to protect the innocent and give the human race a chance to survive. And that includes the beautiful, gutsy Elle who twists him up inside with a single look. The last thing he wants is to take her into a warzone, but soon they are thrown together battling both the alien invaders and their overwhelming attraction. And Marcus will learn just how much he'll sacrifice to keep her safe.

Hell Squad

Marcus

Cruz

Gabe

Reed

Roth

Noah

Shaw

Holmes

Niko

Finn

Theron

Hemi

Ash

Levi

Manu
Also Available as Audiobooks!

Barbarian

Beast

Rogue

Guardian

Cyborg

Imperator

Also Available as Audiobooks!

Hell Squad

Marcus

Cruz

Gabe

Reed

Roth

Noah

Shaw

Holmes

Niko

Finn

Theron

Hemi

Ash

Levi

Manu

Also Available as Audiobooks!

For more information visit AnnaHackettBooks.com

I'm a USA Today bestselling author and I'm passionate about *action romance*. I love stories that combine the thrill of falling in love with the excitement of action, danger and adventure. I'm a sucker for that moment when the team is walking in slow motion, shoulder-to-shoulder heading off into battle. I write about people overcoming unbeatable odds and achieving seemingly impossible goals. I like to believe it's possible for all of us to do the same.

My books are mixture of action, adventure and sexy romance and they're recommended for anyone who enjoys fast-paced stories where the boy wins the girl at the end (or sometimes the girl wins the boy!)

For release dates, action romance info, free books, and other fun stuff, sign up for the latest news here:

Website: www.annahackettbooks.com

Made in United States
North Haven, CT
25 November 2023

44474897R00136